THE SALTWATER CAT

THE SALTWATER CAT

Karen Buck

iUniverse, Inc.

New York Lincoln Shanghai

The Saltwater Cat

iUniverse, Inc.

For information address:
iUniverse, Inc.
2021 Pine Lake Road, Suite 100
Lincoln, NE 68512
www.iuniverse.com

ISBN: 0-595-33289-7

Printed in the United States of America

For my aunt Lola and in memory of my friend, Bethel Wright.

PROLOGUE

▼

Part One

Thump.

Bethel Armstrong lifted her head off the pillow. Now I know I heard something that time, she thought. She reached over to her bed-side table for her glasses, although she wouldn't really need them—here on this sparsely populated part of the North Beach Peninsula in western Washington there were no street lights. It was nothing like their apartment in Chicago, where light streamed in through every window all night long whether they wanted it to or not. The inside of the motor home was inky black.

She turned her face to the other side of the bed, but could see nothing. "George," she whispered, "Did you hear that?"

Silence. She reached over to shake her husband awake, but her hand found only cold, empty sheets. Where was George?

Bethel fumbled for her flashlight and clicked it on. The batteries were weak and it cast just a faint yellow glow into the room. She stepped out of bed and pushed her feet into her slippers.

She groped her way over to the door and flipped the light switch on the wall, but nothing happened. Had George awakened and found the power off? Was he checking the circuit box, or could he be outside? Bethel squeezed the flashlight tighter in her hand, wishing she could wring more light out of it.

"Bethel! Come here right now!" The voice came from the front of the trailer.

"George? Is that you?" Bethel continued to feel her way down the narrow hallway toward the front of the trailer.

She jumped at the sight of a tall, skinny, man, dressed all in black and holding one hand behind his back, a lock of carrot-red hair hanging into his eyes. After a second she recognized Carl Rolley, one of the local men who had befriended her and George soon after they arrived at Seacoast Village. He had always seemed friendly and helpful, but now she found his presence frightening.

"Carl! What are you doing here? Where's George?" Bethel squinted her eyes as his bright flashlight blinded her.

"George needs you to come outside right away. He called me to help him." Carl reached out and began tugging on Bethel's arm. Her flashlight fell to the floor and blinked out. She walked to the door and tried to peer out.

"What is going on, Carl?" She stepped down onto the first step.

Bethel heard, rather than felt, the crushing blow that landed on the back of her head. She lost her balance and fell, cascades of bright bursts of light showering behind her eyelids. Her head hit the steps and her last thought was, "Oh, that was the thump I heard."

Carl Rolley smiled as he reached down and felt for a pulse in Bethel's neck—there was nothing. He stood up and dusted off his hands. Now to bury the remains, he thought, then go home and get some sleep. He grabbed Bethel's ankles and started to pull her body off the porch. "Another day, another dollar," he said, grinning.

Part Two

"But I know my mom and dad wouldn't just leave without telling me where they were going." Amy Sanders let her face fall into her hands. She was unable to stop her tears, but she did not want Sheriff Krupe to see them.

He had not been very helpful so far. He kept telling Amy that lots of people who decided to retire in Seacoast Village changed their minds after their first rain-drenched winter and moved away to a warmer, drier, climate.

"Folks're in and out of here all the time," he said. "Lots of times they just sell their motor homes or whatever and take off."

Amy took a deep shuddering breath. "I believe you about those other people," she said, "but why haven't I heard anything from my parents, especially after they sent me a plane ticket to come and see them?"

Oliver Krupe shrugged, his shirt collar threatening to fold under the rolls of fat around his neck. He tugged it back into place, then patted his holster. Yup, he was still armed and dangerous.

"Beats me. People do funny things, Ms. Sanders. Now, if you'll excuse me, I got important work to do. I have all your information. If I hear anything I'll give you a call."

He watched until Amy had gotten into her rental car and driven away. Then he wiped the sheen of sweat off his face and stood up. "You handled that pretty well, Ollie me boy," he said. "Now you get your reward."

Oliver Krupe, sheriff of the town of Ocean Side, Pacific County, State of Washington, and the most important lawman he knew, headed across the street to the donut shop.

CHAPTER 1

▼

I ran away. With Henry in his carrier and that big rock on my finger, I ran.

Had I really accepted Rick's proposal? Yes, I thought, looking at my left hand again, I had. His shoulders are broad enough to carry any burden I might need help with, I thought. I shook my head and looked down at the black cat sitting next to me.

"So, dumbbell, why are you running away from the man you love?"

"Yow," said Henry, without turning to look at me.

"Good question, cat. But, you don't have to act like that; I'm the dumbbell. So why *am* I running away? After all we went through, Rick and I, uncovering that drug smuggling operation in the veterinary clinic and all of us almost getting killed in the process, you would think I would never want to leave him behind."

Henry just squinted at me. He didn't mind being some place other than home, in fact he seemed to love new adventures, but he wasn't too thrilled about the getting-there part.

I wiggled around in the seat, trying to work the ache out of my back and stop the threatening cramp in the front of my leg. I should have opted for the cruise control. That would have eased the pain of the long day on the road from Spokane.

Spokane was my new old hometown and a place of peace after the devastating end to a marriage I had thought would last forever. Once I had gotten settled, I never imagined I would want to leave Spokane again, but here I was, on my way to my aunt's house in Ocean Side, on the North Beach Peninsula. Lola's place was as far away to the west as I could go without having to cross the water.

In the last months I learned first hand what was said about the best laid plans of mice and men; they tend to go awry. My plans had been to live quietly with my cats and my quilting, trusting nobody with my heart. But then along came Rick Evans.

"Sorry, cat," I said. "Let's take a little detour."

My plans today had been to go directly to Lola's, but instead of turning onto her street, I turned the opposite way, toward the Willapa Bay side of the peninsula. I pulled into a turnout and sat and stared at the water.

Phil Scott had been a knight in shining armor astride a white horse; sweeping me up after graduation from nursing school and carrying me off to Seattle as his bride. Once there, he helped me find my first nursing job. I had eventually been able to make the jump into critical care in the intensive care unit, where I loved working with the critically ill and injured. Phil and I lived in a fabulous townhouse on Queen Anne Hill, one of the best downtown neighborhoods Seattle had to offer, with views of Mt. Rainier to the east, Puget Sound to the west, and downtown with the Space Needle hovering over it to the north. Phil bought me a fancy car and he was happy to adopt Henry, whom I had found wandering about in the parking lot of Seattle Medical Center, and then fluffy little Cleo, who was offered for sale by a scruffy child. We had started to think about having a baby, when to put not too fine a point on it, my life went to shit. Phil started to gamble heavily and then he and a flunky actually physically assaulted me when I could not immediately give Phil the money I was setting aside for our retirement.

That had been bad enough, but I soon discovered that Phil was embezzling money from Home Improvement, Inc., where he was the head accountant. Phil ended up in jail and I sold the townhouse, the fancy car, and as much other stuff as I had been allowed to keep. After the divorce was final I moved back to Spokane.

Seeking peace and quiet, I found a terrific log house in the foothills of Mt. Spokane. Next came a job in a veterinary clinic; my hope being this would be less stressful that working in a people hospital. All Animals Hospital and Crematory was located in a building that originally had housed a funeral home and crematory center on Trent in the Spokane Valley. With the exception of the marble floors and elegant crown molding, it was a typical veterinary clinic. I loved working with the animals and getting to know the owner of the clinic Dr. Brad Mancusco and his partner, Dr. Rick Evans. I thought I was set for a calm, happy, life.

That initial peace was shattered when I found out that Lynda Mancusco, Brad's wife and the clinic bookkeeper, was using the pet crematory and cemetery part of the business to smuggle drugs. With Henry both hindering and helping and with the assistance of the gorgeous Rick Evans, I was able to help get that pipeline shut down. But, lives were lost. Thankfully only one of the good guys died, however.*

Rick and I had worked so closely together that we found ourselves falling in love. When he proposed to me, I accepted. He seemed like the perfect man.

But then, so had Phil. After a couple of months of euphoria with Rick, my feet went beyond cold and became blocks of ice. I needed to get away and do some thinking. The letter from the organizer of the quilt camp on the ocean seemed to be the perfect answer. They needed an instructor for a couple of basic quilting classes and I needed a reason to escape. I packed up supplies, arranged for Rick and a neighbor to watch my house and the animals there, and with Henry in tow, escaped to the west.

* The Crematory Cat, is available from iUniverse at 1-800 823 9235. For a copy signed by the author, see the last page of this book for details

CHAPTER 2

▼

The questions I hoped to avoid for awhile still spun in my head, though. Would Rick change like Phil had? Would we have a couple of good years then would it all go into the toilet?

But, Rick was nothing like Phil, neither physically nor emotionally. While Phil had been just my height, somewhat slight and dark-haired, Rick looked more like a Viking. He had a good four inches of height on me, and I am close to six feet tall myself. His hair is so golden blond that it nearly glistens and his eyes are the blue of glacier ice. My first reaction to him had been "WOW" and he still wowed me every time I saw him. Plus, he seemed to have a caring that, looking back, Phil had lacked.

"So, what should I do, Henry? I'm afraid to grab onto Rick, but I am afraid to lose him, too. I wish you had some advice for me."

Henry was silent. I looked out at the water of Willapa Bay, quiet now with the tide fully in. The quilt seminar where I had been invited to teach was a good chance to clear my head, I hoped. I would take a couple of the classes that sounded interesting, maybe buy some more gadgets for my longarm and custom quilt business, and of course, check out any fabric store I might encounter along the way. Must feed that habit, after all.

Henry looked up at me with a yellow-eyed squint. We had been on the road for almost six hours and he was tired of the confines of his cat carrier. I started the engine and headed back to the road that went to Lola's. It had been years since I had seen her and I was looking forward not only to her coddling me a bit, but some time to walk on the sand and ponder my future.

It had been a very rough time, those first months in the animal clinic. After the dust settled, Rick proposed. He wanted to get married, and so did I, or did I?

The trouble was, the specter of my disastrous marriage to Phil Scott still hovered around me. It had only been a little over a year since I was able to flee Seattle and come home. I knew I loved Rick, but I also knew that I had once loved Phil. His total betrayal, being exposed as an embezzler and a man who would use violence to get what he wanted, had left deep scars. I had thought those scars had healed, but the panic that accepting Rick's ring caused told me they were still there and painful.

"Thank goodness Rick is willing to wait for me to get my head straight," I told Henry as we turned down the street to Lola's house.

He bobbed his head and meowed, he seemed to agree.

CHAPTER 3

▼

"My land, child, it's been too long!" said Lola, greeting me with open arms.

"Yes, it has," I said, hugging her close. My aunt Lola looked the same as always, pleasantly plump with a halo of fluffy white hair escaping the bun on the back of her neck. It was obvious she was my father's sister and no relation to my mother. There was not a hint of snobbery in Lola and my mother was the definition of a snob, seeming to care more about what 'people' thought of her than her own family. I watched Lola as she walked over to the counter and turned on the coffee pot. That hadn't changed, Lola drank coffee night and day like others drank water.

"We'll have a cup ready in no time," she said. "Come and sit down after you let your cat out. I bet he could use a drink of water himself."

I opened the cat carrier and Henry crept out, black shiny body low to the floor. This was a new place; it would need some nosing about before he was comfortable. I watched him ooze around the kitchen, then take a dainty sip from the dish of water Lola put down for him. He slid into the living room, whiskers twitching, ears forward. He would be fine once his survey was done. After all, he was alpha cat wherever he was and he would soon be strutting around on his long slender legs like he owned the place. That had been his personality since he was a kitten. That and his pleasure in people—nobody was a stranger to Henry—his habit of 'killing' odd objects and presenting them to me, and his passion for licking the ears of anybody who picked him up, made him an entertaining companion. But, he was such a softie that if I left him home alone he got so sad wouldn't eat. So, he traveled with me most of the time. His pals the females, fluffy, timid, little Cleo, and the larger, orange, Marmalade, who was not as big as Henry's plump seventeen pounds, but bigger than Cleo's six, were just as happy to stay home. The greyhound, Brandy, didn't like to ride in the car much either, so she stayed home, too. I knew they would be fine. Sully, my neighbor from up the road, and Rick were tending to them while I was gone.

The kitchen in Lola's house hadn't changed either. It still had soft blue paint on the walls and it looked like the cupboards had recently gotten a fresh coat of white paint, they gleamed, and the old pine table shone with a recent waxing.

Lola gleamed too. Her cheeks were pink and she was still wearing those bib aprons she had always favored, dotted with a rainbow of paint dots and smears. Lola was an artist and loved to paint. I had one of her seascapes over my fireplace at home. But, underneath that apron instead of the expected cotton house dress, I saw jeans. Some things do change, after all.

"They decided to rename my place," she said. "They didn't change it a whole lot though, now it's called Lucille's Beach House."

Lola and her husband, Allen, had owned and run Lola's Beach House, a small diner at the edge of the beach, for over 40 years. Lola did most of the work in the diner, while Allen worked for the State of Washington as a road works supervisor. She had loved the cooking and chatting with her customers and had found it hard to sell the business. But, all those years on her feet had taken their toll and she found she could no longer stand in front of a grill or bus tables all day long. After Allen died she knew she couldn't keep things maintained by herself, either.

"So, are you enjoying being retired, Lola?"

"Yeah, Maggie, you know what, I really am. I can paint all day long without feeling guilty, or even just lie in bed if I want to. What's doing with you these days, anyway? I haven't heard much from you recently."

"You knew about my divorce from Phil Scott after he and a buddy assaulted me, right?" Lola nodded. "Well, he is now doing time at the prison in Walla Walla. Then, of course, I wrote to you about the drug smuggling operation I uncovered at the veterinary clinic where I am working. That was really something. Then after that was all over, this happened." I held out my left hand.

"Wow, what a rock! So, who's the new guy?"

"Well…" I stopped to think for a minute. So much to say about Rick, how he seemed to care about me, how gentle and kind he was, how he hadn't tried to push me into bed, where to start? "Rick Evans is one of the veterinarians in the clinic. He and I helped the cops and the DEA expose that drug thing, and in the process of that, plus all the time I spent working with him in the clinic, we fell in love."

Lola sighed. "Sounds heavenly. When is the wedding?"

"That's a tough question, Lola. I'm a little gun-shy, I guess. Phil had seemed like such a nice guy, too, when I first met him. He helped me find my first nursing job, he seemed so honest and true. But, then he changed and I never knew what really happened. Suddenly he demanded the money I had put away for our future and of course you know about him embezzling all that money from Home Improvement, Inc. You know they still haven't found the bulk of that? So now I'm not sure about Rick. Will he change, too?"

CHAPTER 4

▼

Lola and I talked for awhile, then I went in to unpack while she started dinner, happy to be cooking for somebody again. Henry was now walking around her house like he was the king, which of course he knew he was. I called Rick's house and left a message on his answering machine to let him know that I had made it okay.

The next morning I was up early. I could hear the ocean beating on the sand and I could hardly wait to go for a walk. I knew Henry would be anxious to get outside, too. After reading Lilian Jackson Braun's books starring KoKo, the extrasensory Siamese cat with his tolerance of a harness and leash to keep him safe, I decided to see how my cats would do with this. Cleo nearly had a seizure, running madly about the room before I was able to catch her and take the harness off. She had been absolutely terrified. Marmalade didn't seem to mind having the harness put on her, but then she fell over on her side and refused to move. If I set her up her feet she would just tip over again, like a tree being felled. I remembered this behavior from an old tom cat I used to dress up in doll clothes when I was a child. He would lie like a dead thing in the doll buggy, his battle-scarred face surrounded with ruffles. When he had enough, though, he would bail out and run across the lawn, black hairy elbows poking out of puffy sleeves, the dress's skirt trailing behind him across the grass, quite a sight.

This harness idea had been a wash, so far. I wondered how Henry would react. Henry, however, ignored the whole process. He wasn't even interested in smelling the harness, and just shook himself to realign his fur after I put it on him. The tug of the leash he ignored, too. He didn't try to pull away when he reached the end of it, nor did he have one of those twisting fits I have seen leashed cats exhibit. He soon learned that the harness and leash meant an adventure of some sort, whether just to the mail box or into the Blazer for a road trip. He would get as excited as a dog when I picked up his leash.

The only thing that bothered him when we went outside was a dog. Then, he would run toward me to be picked up and rescued, rather than trying to run away. Pretty smart guy. Now I would see how he would do on the beach. I clipped the leash onto the harness and we took off.

Lola's house sat in an ordinary-looking neighborhood. There were houses up and down on both sides of this two-lane road with grass in front and a picket fence or two around the back yards. There were no sidewalks, but wide shoulders of sand made it safe to walk. Except for that sand, the muffled boom of the surf, and the sharp scent of salt in the air, I could have been anywhere. But, the Pacific Ocean was just beyond the back yards of the houses on Lola's side of the street. What I liked the best about Lola's was that I just had to walk out her back door, thread my way a little ways through the coarse dune grass that made up her back yard, and I was on the beach.

Now to see how Henry would react to all this sand and water. We walked across the rough grass to where the sandy beach started. He stopped and stared.

Henry had never seen so much water in his whole life. I had to tug a bit on the leash to get him to move, but he finally stepped out onto the sand. The tide had gone out and the sand was damp. Henry's eyes were a big as quarters and he walked as high on his toes as he could manage, trying to keep his paw pads dry.

We walked out to where the edges of the waves almost reached our feet. The sky was clear, but a faint haze hung in the air, making every direction I looked into a water color painting. A large flock of sand pipers ran about on the sand, picking up little bits of food and chasing the water when it pulled back into the ocean, then running away from the waves as they moved in, their stick-like little legs a blur of motion. A gull hung overhead in the breeze that always blew in off the water, squawking his indignation at the predator I had with me. Henry, not aware of how threatening the gull thought he was, just stared around, eyes dilated to black and nose twitching. I would have loved to have known what he was thinking.

Except for the birds, I was alone on the beach. All I could see to either the right or the left was water, sky, and sand. The North Beach Peninsula boasted twenty-seven miles of uninterrupted beach, one of the longest in the world.

Henry had walked back toward the house and was tugging at his leash. He had had enough of all this water, his expression said. When I turned to head back I saw the lights were on at Lucille's Beach House. "Let's go get some coffee, okay, Henry?"

CHAPTER 5

▼

The outside of the Beach House looked the same as it always had, cedar shakes weathered to silver and an aluminum roof that had become white with dried salt. The front screen door still hung a bit crookedly and the windows that faced the water were steamy around the edges. The only new thing I saw at the little diner that used to be Lola's was the sign. Lucille's, it said now, rather than Lola's. But, the interior was familiar and soothing. The new owners even had a big dog sleeping on the floor at the end of the counter, just like Lola used to have. Hers had been a Heinz-57 mix, this one looked like a St. Bernard.

I slid into my favorite booth, the one with the best view of the ocean. I set Henry next to me on the seat and he pulled himself into his 'I'm a Russian hat' pose, on his chest with front paws tucked away and hips sticking up looking like the hat's ear flaps. He knew dogs, he and Brandy often slept together in Brandy's basket at home, but this dog was an unknown. He kept his eyes fixed on the dozing creature.

"Good morning, what can I get you?"

"Coffee, please, and maybe a little dish of milk for my friend here."

The waitress nodded and walked away, shoulders drooping. She wore a white apron over khaki slacks and a plaid blouse. While the apron may have been crisp and bright when she put it on, it now looked sad and limp. She had light blond hair tied back behind her neck and the fair skin and blue eyes to go with it. There were blue smudges under her eyes, though, and she looked as tired as her apron.

"She looks like she is already worn out, Henry. I remember how hard it is to run this place, though."

The coffee was great, Starbuck's. Henry drank some milk and finally relaxed enough to let his eyes close. The dog had shown no interest in him.

The waitress came back to refill my cup. "Can I get you anything to eat?"

"No, thanks," I told her, "I think my aunt is expecting me for breakfast. Are you Lucille, by chance?"

"No, my name is Amy. I just work here."

"I'm Maggie Jackson and my aunt, Lola Bowen, used to own this place."

"She is really a nice lady," Amy said, her face brightening momentarily. "I think I would have liked working for her."

Amy's voice had a distinctive mid-western twang. "Have you lived out here for very long?" I said.

"Only a couple of months. I came out to visit my parents, but I…" she stopped talking and glanced toward the kitchen. I could see a large, dark-haired woman glaring out at us. She had on the same white apron as Amy, but hers looked so stiffly starched that had she stepped out of it it would have stood on its own. Her hair was pulled back in a tight knot high on her head and she twisted a bar towel in her hands.

"Thank you for coming in. I hope we see you again," Amy said, and hurried off toward the kitchen. I watched her for a minute, then left money on the table for my coffee. Henry and I started back to Lola's house.

"I wonder what that was all about, Henry? He walked casually along the sand with me now, like he had always been a beach cat. "Amy seemed like she was afraid of that woman that we saw in the kitchen." I wondered, was that Lucille? And why was Amy afraid of her?

CHAPTER 6

▼

After breakfast, I decided to check out where the quilt seminar was to be held. I wanted to make sure I knew where I was going so I wouldn't be late the next day for the class I was scheduled to teach.

Henry was curled up on my bed, fast asleep. I left him to his nap and hopped in the Blazer.

The Seacoast Inn had started life as a gambling casino. Native American tribes had done very well supporting their tribal way of life with casinos throughout the state of Washington and the little town of Ocean Side, snuggled into the dunes between Ocean Park and Long Beach, Washington, seemed an ideal spot for another casino. So, a couple of years earlier during the winter months, a casino with an attached motel was built in Ocean Side. It opened in the spring and the first six months were great. The people came in droves and the money flowed in.

But, with the end of the tourist season the money dried up. Many of the people who lived around the small North Beach Peninsula towns made the bulk of their income during the spring and summer months, mostly from tourist dollars. This money had to sustain them through the lean winter months and they had little to spare for gambling. The rich tourists had fled as the winter rains started, taking all their discretionary cash with them. The casino folded after its first year.

A company that ran conventions and seminars bought the building and remodeled it into a center for conferences and conventions, with lots of space for meetings. People could stay right at the site in the adjoining motel rooms, which made The Seacoast Inn attractive for retreats and get-togethers of all kinds. Its cavernous gambling hall had been converted into comfortable-size meeting rooms and they were now busy year round. The Washington Longarm Guild was having its annual meeting there this year. Local interest had been even greater than expected, and while the conference was supposed to be just for the longarm quilter, so many local people had expressed interest in quilting in general that the local quilt group sponsoring the meeting decided to offer a beginning quilting class. That was the one I was asked to come and teach.

Glad for the chance to put some thinking time between Rick and me, I jumped at the opportunity. Being able to stay with Lola and spend some time with her was an added benefit.

I passed Lucille's Beach House on my way to Seacoast Village. Amy was out in front, sweeping the walk. She looked up at the toot from my horn. I waved, but she turned her face to the ground and continued her sweeping. I could see the large woman standing in one of the windows, watching Amy sweep. Amy looked almost frightened. What was going on there, anyway?

C H A P T E R 7

▼

The next day I stood in front of the group of ladies what would make up my class for the next couple of days. It is always so much fun to introduce new people to quilting, to take away their fears of combining colors and of design. There have even been a few men take my classes in the past. They tended to be the bravest quilters of all, not afraid to push the envelope when it came to color and pattern.

"I'm glad to see you all brought sewing machines with you today. As you know, this class is four hours long, one hour this morning, one hour this afternoon, and the rest in a two-hour session tomorrow. By the time we get done tomorrow you will have completed at least one nine patch quilt block and hopefully you will also have the courage and information to make a whole quilt!" I looked over the class. I was glad I had planned for a large group and brought enough cut fabric to make 20 quilt blocks, all but one of the 20 spaces were filled.

"First, we are going to talk a bit about quilting. The most important thing about a quilt is that other than using a quarter-inch seam and pre-washing your fabrics, there are no rules. You can make a quilt any color, size, or pattern combination you want. This is your piece of art and don't let anybody tell you otherwise! All-cotton fabric is the best, polyester, knits, and polyester blends can shrink and stretch in funny ways, so stay away from those. You don't need to spend a lot of money on fabric, remember, our ancestors used to make wonderful quilts out of scraps of clothing and cloth flour sacks. Just learn what a good fabric feels and looks like. I have even found some great stuff on the sale tables of fabric shops for a dollar a yard. Go to the quilt shops, there are lots of them around. Spend some time looking at and touching fabric, and buy, of course! You will soon know what is quality and what is not. You will be amazed what you can find and where you can find it.

"Lecture over. Let's get quilting! To save you time, I have cut out the pieces needed to make one nine patch block. Go to the table and select five squares of one dark color from the table on the left and four squares of one light color from the table on the right."

I watched the women hurry to the tables, reminding me of the sand pipers on the beach as they hurried back and forth, trying to find their ideal pattern and color choices. When they were finally back at their seats I started the instructions that would show them how to make their nine patch block.*

When my class was over I spent some time looking at the vendors' displays. I was enchanted to see a longarm machine with a short table, about six feet in length. That would be great for someone who did not have the space I did. It used the same principle as my big machine. The quilt top, batting and back were pinned together then secured to two long rollers, one across the front of the table, one across the back. Then, most of the quilt layers were rolled up on one of the rollers, and pulled taut. I always rolled the quilt onto the front roller then rolled the finished part onto the back roller, but like with so many other things in quilting, there was more than one right way to do it.

The sewing machine itself, mounted on tracks, was "driven" over the exposed part of the quilt, sewing all the while. The quilted portion was then rolled up onto the roller and more of the unquilted part of the quilt was ready to be sewn on. Because of the way the track system was assembled, it was possible to go in all directions with the sewing head. Curves, swirls, loop-de-loops, it was all possible. I believed the person who told me that it could take 10 hours to pick out what it took 10 seconds to sew in, though. One could get in trouble in a hurry. Longarm quilting seemed like a combination of dancing and ditch digging, hard work, but with something to show for it at the end.

I thought about Killer Quilts, my studio at home in Spokane. The house I had been lucky enough to buy had an attached shop that became a perfect quilt studio. The table part of my Noltings longarm quilting machine is 14 feet long, but fits easily in that large space. There is plenty of space for my regular sewing machines, too, and I was able to add three large tables for cutting and pinning. I teach an occasional small class at the shop, and with the addition of folding chairs there is room for people to bring and use their own machines. In one corner is a fat, pot-bellied, gas stove. I put a cushy chair on each side of it and on a chilly day it is a perfect spot to curl up under a quilt with a book, a cup of something warm, and maybe a cookie or two.

I hoped that Cleo and Marmalade, the other two cats, and Brandy, the dog, were doing okay without me. Sully, my wild-haired neighbor from up the road, was going to take my mail in and feed them, and Rick would check in from time to time too, so they should be okay. Now, if I could just get Henry to eat when I wasn't there I wouldn't have to always haul him with me. I looked over to where he was keeping watch on all that was going on. The leash was attached to his harness and fixed to a table leg so that if something startled him he wouldn't be able to run away and risk getting lost.

Speaking of eating, my stomach was grumbling. I looked at my watch; no wonder I was hungry, it was after one.

* instructions for a nine patch quilt block are at the end of this book

CHAPTER 8

▼

When I got back to Lola's I found the house empty. I dished up some food for Henry and decided to go back to Lucille's Beach House for lunch, hoping for a chance to talk to Amy again. She was not there, however. The large woman had been joined by a hulking man, whom she called Tiny. His shoulders were stooped and hands as big as rump roasts reached almost to his knees. From where I sat his eyes looked like black holes in his face. He was wearing jeans and a white T shirt covered with an apron. A paper chef's hand perched on buzz cut red hair. He was doing the cooking and when he yelled, "Order up, Lucille," I knew I was seeing the new owners of my aunt's diner.

Lucille plopped a large bowl of clam chowder in front of me. Ah. I sat for a moment luxuriating in the aroma of clams swimming in a creamy soup. I could see bits of bacon and cubes of potato, too, with just a spattering of corn, perfect.

The chowder tasted as wonderful as it looked. I had to restrain myself from licking the bowl. The fish and chips that followed were equally good, the breading thin and crisp on the fish and the potatoes not overly greasy. Even the tartar sauce was homemade and delicious. Whatever else about Lucille and Tiny, they did know how to cook. The diner was busy, too. Obviously I was not the only one who liked the food. I left my money on the table with the bill and started back to Lola's.

Henry was still alone at Lola's when I got there. He greeted me with a glad squawk and climbed up my front when I picked him up. He clamped his paws around my neck and stuck his nose in my ear and purred so loudly I could feel my brain jiggle. The ocean was calling to me again and Henry probably needed to find a place to dig in the dirt. I peeled him off my chest and put his harness on him and we went out to walk in the sand again.

After our walk I sat down in a comfy lawn chair in Lola's back yard. She and Allen hadn't even tried to grow a lawn—the salt water that blew up into the yard killed regular grass. They just kept the beach grass mowed down and poured a cement slab to serve as a patio. Henry was quite happy to sit on the table next to me and survey his new domain.

I must have nodded off, as the next thing I noticed was that the light in the sky had faded. Henry had crawled into my lap at some point; he was asleep there now, nose tucked under a curled paw. Looking back over my shoulder, I could see Lola moving around in the kitchen. She was probably cooking dinner. Rousing Henry, I got up to go in and help her.

"So, what do you know about Lucille and Tiny...is that her husband?" We were sitting by the fire in Lola's living room, dinner settling in our stomachs. One of the frequent costal showers had come in while we ate, putting a chill in the air. Water gurgled in the gutter downspouts and Henry sat on the wide bay window seat, watching the wind-tossed rain drops hit the glass and slide down.

"I don't know a whole lot about them, but yes, Tiny is Lucille's husband," Lola said. "Their last name is Rolley and his real name is Percy." She chuckled. "Doesn't exactly fit him, does it?"

"Not even close," I said, "No wonder he has a nickname, but Tiny doesn't seem to be right either. Is he as mean as he looks?"

"You know, I don't really know them all that well. They seemed pleasant enough while we were negotiating on the sale of the Beach House, but they really had to be nice then, didn't they? They have a son, Carl, who has given them some grief, I do know that."

"I just wondered. I was in there early yesterday morning and talked a bit to a waitress of theirs, Amy. She seemed almost afraid of Lucille."

Lola sighed. "Amy. She has been a bit of a trial to the folks here in Ocean Side. Her parents moved here a year or so ago, George and Bethel Armstrong are their names, I think. Amy showed up a couple of weeks ago claiming they had invited her to come and stay with them, but when she got here they were gone. She's been all over trying to find them."

"Where did they go?"

"We don't know, Maggie. We tried to convince Amy that lots of times people come here to retire, but don't realize what the weather is like, or the fact that there is little to do here during the winter months. Frequently people just pack up and leave after that first year."

"But, if Amy's parents invited her to come stay with them—wouldn't they have let her know if they were going to leave?"

"That part does bother me some," said Lola. But, Sheriff Krupe investigated and said things looked fine to him."

I lay in bed that night, thinking about Amy and her parents. Maybe that was why she looked so sad. But, if they *had* moved away why hadn't they let her know? Maybe she left home before they could get in touch with her; maybe there is a letter waiting for her, or a message on her voice mail. Had she checked? I turned over, restless. I was going to have to find out, have to talk to her, damn it. When it came to trouble, I always felt there were two kinds of people in the world, those who jumped toward it and those who jumped away. As an RN, I was always willing to jump toward a person in medical trouble, but that tendency seemed to have overlapped into my regular life, as well. The last time I jumped toward trouble I ended up locked in an animal cage, facing certain death, and it had been Henry who had saved the day.

That was a whole different thing, I decided. I *knew* there was criminal activity going on then, this was just an unhappy young woman who might need some help. It couldn't hurt to talk to her, now could it?

CHAPTER 9

▼

I got up early again. I took Henry for a quick walk, then got in the Blazer. I would breakfast at Lucille's and maybe get a chance to talk to Amy.

The lights were on in the diner and I could smell the seductive aroma of bacon. I went in and sat down, once again the only customer.

"You want coffee?" Lucille was standing by my table, holding a steaming pot.

"Sure," I told her, turning my cup right side up. "And could I see a menu, too, please?"

"Breakfast is listed on the board," she said, pointing to her left. "You new around here? I've not seen you around before the last couple of days."

"No, I'm not exactly new. I'm Maggie Jackson, my aunt is Lola Bowen and I'm just here for a visit. I understand you bought this place from her."

"Yes, we did, about three years ago. Nice to meet you, Maggie. I'm Lucille Rolley, but I guess you already knew that."

We chatted a bit, but when I asked her about Amy, her face changed.

"Amy works the late shift today. She won't be in until two this afternoon. Why are you wondering about her?"

"I chatted with her a bit the other day and she seemed so sad. I hope she is okay."

Lucille frowned. "If I were you I'd stay away from her. She's been trying to stir up trouble around here."

"Really? What about?"

The bell over the door pinged with another customer and Lucille walked away, looking relieved. "Enjoy your breakfast," she said.

At the longarm conference I took a couple of classes to learn some new quilting techniques, then went to teach my own class. My students were so excited; they were starting to see what their nine patch quilt blocks were going to look like. It was fun to watch them bend their brains around new meanings for words like square, block, sash, border, frame, and binding. They sewed, pressed, picked out mistakes, and re-sewed; they were having a blast.

"Okay, now tomorrow," I told them, "You will finish your blocks and I'll show you some different ways to make lots of blocks like this into a quilt. You already have the instructions on how to make these blocks quickly, so you can make more blocks of your own and do a whole quilt if you want to. See you tomorrow."

It was another half an hour before I could get away, so many of the students had questions or just wanted to chat. By the time I got back to Lola's I was ready for another nap in her lawn chair. But first, Henry needed his walk.

CHAPTER 10

▼

Henry was standing by the door, waiting to go out. I slipped his harness over his head and he was ready. He ran out to the full extent of his leash while I was closing the door. He dug a hole in the sand and squatted over it, then carefully buried his deposit. I set a piece of driftwood on the spot then put a rock on top of it. I would clean up his little mess when we got back from our walk.

While just the day or two before he had been leery of the ocean water, coming and going like it did, now he was totally in control of this, his new kingdom. He chased the surf back out toward the ocean, then skittered back to me when the waves pushed their way back up the beach. The wet sand didn't even seem to bother him. He had conquered it. I watched him play, thinking again how very Siamese he looked. I had heard that all short-haired black cats were related to the usually distinctively marked Siamese, and looking at him certainly reinforced that. While the only other color than black he wore were the white hairs in his ears, his body was pure Siamese: long, graceful legs, tall pointed ears framing a triangular face, and even a kink at the end of his skinny, rope-like tail. His eyes were a golden yellow that sometimes became a greenish-yellow shade, changing depending on his mood, but they were not crossed. I was glad about that; I always felt a bit off balance looking into crossed cat eyes. He lacked the raucous voice of the Siamese, thank goodness, but could put up a pretty good noise if he wanted to. He liked his Deli Cat, too, his slightly plump tummy said.

We walked for a ways down the beach, watching the waves curl and drop their tops on the sand. Henry danced on the end of his leash, batting at pieces of seaweed and poking his sharp nose into pieces of shell that littered the sand. I was getting a little tired of the wind in my face, so even though Henry was pulling hard on his leash trying to go further up the peninsula, I picked him up and turned around to head back. Usually he liked being carried, but today he struggled and kicked.

"Okay, big guy, you can just walk," I said, putting him down. But instead of continuing down the beach, he turned back the way we had come then headed for the tules and the waving dune grass, pulling all of leash from the reel.

"Come on, kitty, that is somebody else's place. Let's go back to Lola's."

But he ignored me and pulled hard against his leash, trying to crawl under a large piece of driftwood. At home he liked to "kill" things and present them to me for my approval. He would pick up such sundries as an empty toilet paper tube, a rubber band, a crumpled piece of paper, whatever struck his fancy. At home he had a whole box of odd items to chose from. He would bring the item to me, making a funny series of moaning, grunting, and snarking noises. I learned to not ignore him when he did this, as occasionally he brought me a mouse, usually still alive. If I didn't go get whatever he brought me and tell him what a good kitty he was, he would just drop the item and walk away. That was okay for a toilet paper tube, but not such a good idea with a terrified mouse.

I could hear the moaning noises; he must have found some prey for me.

"Good kitty, good boy, what did you find?" I could feel my grin, he was such a funny cat. I took a few steps his way to give him some more leash.

Sand flew out around the end of the driftwood log as he tried to dig himself underneath. I walked over to him and froze. Instead of a scrap of paper or some such bit of beach detritus, I could see a motionless hand lying palm up in the sand near where Henry was digging.

I clambered around the driftwood and there was Amy, lying crumpled in the sand. I dropped to my knees and reached for her arm. She had a pulse. It was a bit thready, but her heart was beating in a steady rhythm. I looked at her face again. Now I saw the purplish goose-egg-sized lump above her right eye and the trickle of blood that ran down her temple. I jumped to my feet and look wildly around. I needed some help.

Lola's house was too far away. I fastened the leash reel to the driftwood. Henry would be okay—he had stopped his wild digging and was sitting next to Amy licking her arm. I ran to the house on the dune. I banged on the door, but there was nobody home. The house on the other side didn't show any signs of life either and I realized these were weekend retreats that sat empty most of the time. I dashed out onto the beach and looked up and down it. Nobody else was out for an afternoon stroll.

I ran back to Amy. She was starting to move around a little bit and seemed to be coming to. I told her I'd be right back and went up to the house where I had knocked. Through the kitchen window I could see the phone on the wall. Hoping it was connected, I took a deep breath; I was going to break and enter.

The homeowner had bordered a sidewalk with rocks and I picked one up to throw through the glass. But, just before I let it fly, I decided to check the windows I could reach. I was amazed when one of them slid up when I pushed on it. Good. Now I didn't have to break, just enter.

I wiggled through the opening and ran for the phone. The peninsula was not yet part of the 911 system, so I just dialed O and told the operator where I was and that I needed help. I crawled back out the window and pulled it shut to keep the salt air out of the house and went to Amy.

She was sitting up against the driftwood now and I could see where she had been sick in the sand. She at least had a concussion; I just hoped she did not also have a fractured skull.

Time crept by and finally I heard a siren. A sheriff's car pulled up and a heavy-set man pulled himself out of the front seat and waddled over to us.

"What's the big problem, here, anyway? Who are you?"

"My name is Maggie Jackson. My aunt is Lola Bowen. I was just taking my cat for a walk on the beach and we found Amy lying here unconscious. I'm afraid she may have a concussion. We need to get her to…"

The big man cut me off. "What makes you such a hotshot, anyway? This is my jurisdiction and I'll decide what needs to be done." He turned to Amy and hitched up the wide leather belt holding his handcuffs and pistol. "What are you doing down here, anyway?"

She looked up at him, eyes glazed. "I don't remember. I was on my way to work and then…" She turned her hands up and shrugged.

"What difference does it make why she is here?" I asked, nearly jumping up and down with impatience. "This woman is injured and needs medical attention. Is there an ambulance coming?"

The fat man turned to me, his little pig eyes shooting sparks. "I decide if we need an ambulance here or not. She looks fine to me, though." He leaned down to Amy. "Why don't you just get your ass outa the sand and get going." He grabbed Amy's arm and twisted it, trying to pull her to her feet.

"She has suffered head trauma," I said, trying to sound as severe as I could. I could not understand why this man, who must be a policeman of some sort, judging by his uniform, was being so difficult. "She needs to be moved as carefully as possible to someplace where a doctor can take a look at her and make sure there is nothing seriously wrong. She could have a serious head or neck injury."

"It's just a little bump—why don't you butt out?" He was glaring at me, now.

"I'm a nurse and I'm worried about Amy."

"Well, you just go ahead and worry, then. I got things to do." He released Amy's arm, walked to his car, got in and drove away.

Stunned, I stood and watched him go. Ocean Side Police Department, it said on the car door. I would be talking to this man's boss, come the next day. Now, though, I needed to get Amy off the beach and find her some medical attention.

"Do you think you can walk?" I asked her. It wouldn't be the best thing for her, but it didn't look like there would be any choice. I didn't want to risk leaving her alone while I went for the Blazer; I was afraid she might become confused and wander off.

Henry had sat quietly the entire time, but now he was ready to move, too. I helped Amy to stand up, she was fairly stable on her feet. Slowly we started up the beach toward Lola's, Amy leaning on my arm.

CHAPTER 11

▼

It took us several minutes to get to Lola's, but by the time we got to the house Amy was walking without any trouble. Her eyes had cleared and she knew where she was and what was going on.

Once inside, I had her sit down and I ran for my car keys. She needed to be seen by a doctor right away.

"I don't want to go to the hospital," she said. "I feel fine, really." She stood up to go, but swayed on her feet and sat back down. "I'll be okay after I rest for a minute. I need to get to work."

"No, Amy, I don't think you'd better try to go anywhere. You have a head injury and it could get worse." I turned to my aunt. "Lola, do you know a doctor who might be willing to see Amy today at his office?"

"My doctor, Owen Grant, is on vacation for the next two weeks, but I don't think he was going to leave town. He still has patients in the hospital he needs to look after. Let me try him." She went to the phone.

"Thanks, Owen," I heard her say. "We'll be expecting you."

"He's going to come over here," Lola said. "Let's get Amy comfortable while we wait for him."

We settled Amy in Lola's big recliner in the living room and gave her a glass of water. Lola went to the kitchen to put some ice in a bag.

Amy sipped water. "I can't thank you enough, Maggie," she said. "I remember meeting you at the Beach House, but how did you find me today?"

"My cat actually is the one that found you. What happened to you, anyway?"

"I don't know. I was walking home from the Beach House and the next thing I knew I was lying in the sand and a cat was licking my arm." She winced when

Lola laid the cloth-wrapped ice bag on her forehead, but then reached up to hold it in place herself.

"Thank you," Amy said, "That feels pretty good."

A knock on the door interrupted her. Lola went to answer the knock.

"This is Owen Grant," said Lola, leading a tall, husky, man into the room. "He's my doctor. Owen, this is my niece, Maggie Jackson."

Dr. Grant was an older man with a no-nonsense air. He was wearing jeans and a plaid shirt and carried a little black bag, just like every country doctor I ever imagined. He nodded to me and went straight to Amy. Lola and I went to the kitchen to wait.

After a few minutes he came out and sat down at the table.

"Well, she's a lucky girl. She took a pretty hard knock on the head, but luckily it just rang her bell a little bit—there's no fracture that I can determine without an x-ray. What happened to her?"

I told him the little that I knew. He frowned. "It looks to me like she was hit with a brick. I found bits of red crumbly material in the wound when I washed it out. Where did you say you found her, Maggie?"

"I can't tell you exactly; I'd have to show you. I had just started back from a walk up the beach when Henry went nuts and started to dig in the sand by a piece of driftwood. The house had bluish trim, I think, and it was one of a group of five or six houses. Maybe a half a mile up the peninsula from here?"

Owen nodded. "I think I know the place you mean. I'm going to go up and take a look around. I'll be right back."

Lola and I watched him maneuver his four-wheel-drive SUV down the driveway next to her house and out onto the sand. With the tide out, the sand would be firm enough to keep him from bogging down. I am too timid to drive on the beach. Even though is it not logical, I am convinced the tide will suddenly come in and get me. This seemed to happen at least once a year to somebody who left their car sitting too long in the sand at low tide and not too long ago in Spokane I had read about a couple that drowned when they got caught in the tide while digging clams. Owen could drive; I would wait at Lola's. It would be a quick trip in a car for him to get back to where I had found Amy lying in the sand.

Lola and I sat down at the table to wait. "But who would do this, Maggie?" asked Lola. "Are you sure she didn't just fall and hit her head?"

I shook my head. "I don't know. I don't remember seeing any bricks near where I found her, but I really didn't spend much time looking around, either. Hopefully Dr. Grant will find something."

After only a few minutes, Owen Grant pulled his SUV off the beach, parked by Lola's house and came back into the kitchen.

"So what did you find? Do you think she fell and hit her head?" I asked him.

"It would be hard to be positive from the wound, it could have happened either way, on purpose or by accident," he said, "But, there are no rocks or bricks anywhere around where you found her that would have left behind the kind of residue I found in her scalp wound. Besides, there were no footprints in the sand that were the size of her feet—just lots of stirred up sand. It looks to me like she was carried out and dumped there and whoever did it stirred up the sand to cover up their tracks."

A cold finger of fear slid down my back. The beach had always been a refuge for me, now it felt foreign, dark, and scary.

Lola walked Dr. Grant to the door. "Amy should be fine. She just needs to rest and she shouldn't be alone tonight," he said.

"She can stay here tonight and we'll watch her," I heard Lola say. "Thanks for coming over."

Lola and I helped Amy settle into one of the guest bedrooms with a fresh bag of ice. I set my alarm clock. Amy would need to be wakened every two hours until morning to assess her mental status and make sure she wasn't having any problems with the concussion getting worse.

Lola had made coffee and it smelled wonderful. We sat and sipped at her kitchen table. "Tell me again where you found her, Maggie."

After I finished she nodded. "Yes, I know that spot. It's a good thing you found her when you did. The tide could have washed her out to sea; it comes clear up to the base of those dunes this time of the year."

"But who in the world could have done this to her, and why? Do you think it has anything to do with her parents disappearing?"

Lola looked worried. "There's been a lot of talk recently about funny things going on, but the sheriff checks them all out and says things are fine. I do wonder, though."

"What does the sheriff look like, Lola? Is he a fat toad with little mean eyes?"

Lola laughed. "Sounds like you've met Oliver Krupe. He's quite a gem." Her laugh turned to a snort of disgust. "This is such a small area and we have such a small tax base, we just can't afford to hire a really top-notch policeman. He is the only sheriff for the whole peninsula, at least as far down as Ilwaco. The sheriff's office is here in Ocean Side because there is a big, fancy, old, building a developer had restored and Oliver felt it best exemplified the status of the office." She spun her hand in the air, mimicking a royal wave, sarcasm dripping from her voice.

"In some ways he's good, though," she went on, "He can really direct the traf-fic we get during the Rod Run to the End of the World they have in Ocean Park every Labor Day weekend."

If that was all the good that Lola could think of to say about Sheriff Krupe, then this guy was clearly worthless. She rarely had a bad thing to say about any-body.

CHAPTER 12

▼

The next morning I drove to the sheriff's office. This Oliver Krupe's behavior was not that of a professional law enforcement person. Here I go, I thought, sticking my nose in again, but I needed to talk to his boss.

When I pulled up to the Town Hall I sat for a minute and stared. The Town Hall was a part of a grandiose block-long brick building. Lola told me a developer whose eyes were bigger than his brain thought that he could create a booming metropolis here; start up a town that would be all his. But, Ocean Park, Ocean Side, and Long Beach had been in existence for many years with plenty of room to grow and each with lots of tourist attractions, too. There was really no need for another small town. The developer's money had run out just about the time he finished what he envisioned as the first block of an old-time main street lined with businesses, offices, stores, and all the other places where tourists could be tempted to leave some money. The block was lovely, I would give him that. It was made up of the one stylish old building, with tall windows in each store front. Gargoyles grinned down from all four corners of the block, looking down on a wide boardwalk that ran the full length of the building. He had restored it beautifully, but a throbbing business center it was not. There was a boutique full of tourist gizmos, a coffee shop, the Town Hall, the sheriff's office and a Real Estate office with fly-specked windows, but the last three spaces stood empty, staring dully out over the board sidewalk that went across the front of the building. I went to the sheriff's office and stepped inside.

The woman sitting at the desk just inside the door looked like she could be Oliver Krupe's twin sister. She had the same little, mean, pig eyes and if she smiled I imagined her face would crack.

"Help you?" she said.

"Who is in charge of this office?" I asked.

"I am, what's it to you?" Oliver Krupe stepped out of his office, his hand on the butt of the gun that jutted out from the hip that bulged below his belt.

Oops. No luck here. "I thought I would need to come and fill out a report about what happened on the beach yesterday," I said.

"What for?" he asked. "That Sanders woman is okay, isn't she?"

"Yes, she seems to be, but Dr. Grant said that he is pretty sure that somebody hit her in the head and I assumed you would be investigating."

"Well, you assumed wrong," he said, sneering. "There is nothing to investigate, she just fell, that's all."

"But, Dr. Grant said…"

"I don't much give a crap about what Dr. Grant said. I say it was an accident, so be it. There's nothing to investigate and I suggest you mind your own business."

I stared at Sheriff Krupe. He glared back at me, daring me to argue. The woman at the desk, Judi, her name tag said, looked at me with the same expression. There would be no point pressing the issue, I could see that. I turned and left the office.

By the time I got back to Lola's she had lunch ready. Amy was sitting at the table and only the dark bruise on the side of her face and scrape on her head was proof that anything at all had happened the day before.

"How are you feeling?" I asked her.

"Much better this morning. I had a bearcat of a headache when I woke up, but a couple of Tylenol really helped. But, I'm afraid I'll lose my job; Lillian doesn't allow any unplanned absences."

"I could go talk to her and…"

"No!" Amy said, looking scared. "I can get another job. I don't want to make her any more mad at me than she probably already is."

I sat and looked at Amy for a minute. "Well, what can I do to help?"

Her eyes filled with tears. "All I want to know is where my parents are. I've asked all around and nobody can seem to help me."

"I assume you've talked to the sheriff?" I said.

She nodded her head. "He was the worst. He told me people come out here to live all the time, then change their minds and go back where they came from. I wanted to file a missing persons report, but he refused to take it; he tore it up in front of my face."

If I hadn't seen firsthand what a poor excuse for a cop this Sheriff Krupe was, I might have wondered about Amy's story. She sounded almost hysterical. But, I had met the man and I could believe every word she said. I looked at my watch—I needed to get to the Seacoast Inn to teach the last session of my quilt class.

"Amy, I need to go, but I'll be back in a couple of hours. Try to remember everything you have done and everybody you have talked to you about your folks and we can talk about it when I get back."

She grabbed my arm. "You'll help me? Oh, Maggie, thank you so much!"

"I don't know what I'll be able to do, but I'll give it a shot. I'll see you later," I said, "Get some rest while I'm gone."

NOW what was I getting myself into?

CHAPTER 13

▼

I spent the last class showing my students how many different effects they could get with basic nine-patch blocks by arranging them in various ways. They were amazed at all the wonderful designs they could get with this simple block. Even though I thoroughly enjoyed the time I spent with all of them, I was glad when the class was over and the last straggler had packed up her machine and left. I was anxious to get back to Lola's and hear Amy's story.

"Your aunt gave me a notebook and I tried to write down everything I could remember," Amy said. We were sitting out on the patio and watching the ocean as we talked. Henry was curled up in her lap, safe in his harness.

"Tell me everything you remember," I said.

"Well, my parents' names are George and Bethel Armstrong. He's not actually my dad, my real dad, Benjamin Sanders, died about 10 years ago and my mom married George a few years after that. George has been like a real father to me, though, and I love him almost as much as I did my own dad. Anyway, they decided to move out here where they could be close to the ocean. Both of them had spent most of their lives in Chicago, right in the city, and really wanted to live someplace that wasn't so crowded. They had friends whose kids lived in Long Beach and they had seen pictures of the area. Sort of suddenly they sold their apartment, packed up all their stuff, and bought a big travel trailer; it is more like a mobile home, actually. They got a truck to pull it, hitched their car to the back of the trailer, and headed west. I had a job I liked and also had a boyfriend at that time, so I decided not to come with them.

"They didn't find any property they liked around Long Beach, so they came to Ocean Side where they found a great spot with an ocean view. They were so happy. My mother send me pictures and wrote and invited me to come out and spend some time with them this summer. I'm a teacher and don't have to do any summer classes until closer to the start of school. Besides, I had just broken up with Sammy, he was my boyfriend. I had caught him fooling around with another woman, so I planned on spending at least a month here, both to visit my parents and to just get away. My mom was so excited about my coming she even sent me a plane ticket.

"I got here about two weeks ago. I rented a car at the airport in Portland and drove up that same day. I have a map my mother sent me showing me where their place was. I carry it with me all the time."

Amy dug around in her pocket and pulled out a folded piece of typing paper. I unfolded it and saw a very clear hand-drawn map showing just which road the Armstrong's place was on and where to turn to get there.

"So you were able to find their place okay?"

"Yes. It was just how it shows on this map. But, when I got there it was just a vacant lot. I could see where there had been a trailer parked, there was a new-looking concrete pad, but that was all. Not even the mailbox by the road had their name on it anymore."

"So, then what did you do?"

"Well, I thought I must have somehow gone the wrong way. I went a little ways down the main road and stopped in Ocean Park at a store called Jack's. What a fabulous general-type store that is; they have everything there. I asked a lady who worked there to tell me where this property was, based on the map I had. She told me to go where I had just been, that that was the only spot like that around here."

"You must have been in a panic," I said.

"Yes, I was. I didn't know what to do next, but when I went out to get back in the car I remembered the Sheriff's office I saw when I drove through Ocean Side. I decided to go there and see if anybody could help me."

"And we already know what kind of response you got. What did you do next?"

"Well, I didn't bring a lot of money with me, but I was able to find a room that I could afford in a sort of a boarding house. Then I went job hunting. I wasn't going to leave until I knew what happened to my parents and I knew I'd need some money to live on. I have a little savings back home, but didn't really want to use that up unless I had to. I was able to get on at Lillian's Beach House and while it didn't pay much, it was enough. But now, of course, I'll have to start all over."

"Did you talk to anybody else except the sheriff about your parents?"

Amy nodded. "As soon as I could, I went around and talked to the families that live the closest to my parents' place. None of them could tell me anything except that one day my folks were there and the next day they were gone. But, I had a hard time even getting that much information. It almost seemed like people were afraid to talk to me about my parents."

"So everything had disappeared overnight, the trailer and all, huh?"

"Oh, no, not at all. I found out that everything was still there the next day after my parents were gone. Then a local guy, Carl Rolley, started cleaning out the trailer and selling the things that were inside. When everything was gone, he sold the trailer, too."

"How could he do that? Had they signed the title over to him?"

"I had a really hard time getting a chance to talk to him, but that's finally what he told me. He wouldn't show me any proof, though. He said they told him he could just have everything and sell it for whatever he could get for it. He said they didn't even care about the money."

"Have you told the sheriff about all this new info you got, too?"

"Oh, yes, and I got the same response again, to just go away and stop causing trouble. Excuse me, I'll be right back."

Amy handed Henry to me and got up and went into the house. I sat and stared at the water. This was the most insane story I had ever heard. How could any lawman brush off what looked so suspicious? I was starting to wonder about that lawman.

When Amy came back out she looked exhausted. "That's enough for today; you look really tired," I said. "Why don't you go take a nap and we can talk later. Maybe I'll go talk to those neighbors you mentioned."

"Keep the map for now so you know where to go. I think you're right; I do need to lie down. My headache is coming back," Amy said. I watched her go back into the house, defeat obvious in the slump of her shoulders.

"Well, Henry, what do you think? Shall I go ask some questions?" He just squinted at me. "You need to stay here, though. C'mon." I took him and settled him down next to Amy, who was already asleep. "I'll be back pretty soon," I told him. He just bobbed his head in reply.

CHAPTER 14

▼

My aunt Lola had really entered the modern age. There was a shiny fax machine sitting on her antique desk and a computer on a newer desk in the corner. I used the fax machine to make a copy of Amy's map; I did not want to risk losing the original.

On the bottom of the map Amy had written down the neighbor's names. That would make my task easier, as I didn't really know how to go about this. Just knock on doors and ask, I guess.

It was easy to find the Armstrong's home site. Just like Amy had said, it had a great view of the ocean, but was far enough back to be safe from the water. I could see why they had liked it there. I looked at the list she had made again. It read:

Grace and Ralph Bunbred—retired couple
Hester and Sylvia Olsen—spinster sisters
Dick and Eve Medcaff—young couple, he rents horses for tourists to ride on the beach
Frank Ottman and Barry, his son—they have a huge vegetable garden
Mavis O'Reilly—ceramics artist, she has a shop in her house

I parked the Blazer and looked around. There was a dainty little woman clipping roses from a hedge that ran all around her house just across the street from Amy's parents' place. This was probably either Grace, Hester, or Sylvia. Amy had said that both Eve and Mavis were young women. I started across the street.

"Gracie?" An elderly man hobbled out onto the porch. "Do you know where my glasses are? I've looked everywhere."

"Try the top of your head, Ralph," she said, smiling at me as I got closer to her yard.

"Oh, drat," he said, "That's the only place I didn't look." He turned and went back in the house.

"Hello," she said. "Can I help you with anything?"

"Hi," I said. "My name is Maggie Jackson, my aunt is Lola Bowen?" I knew that most of the year-round people in Ocean Side knew each other and Lola's husband, Allen, had been a well-known town personality.

"Oh, yes, of course. How nice to met you. Maggie, you said?"

Good, she was smiling. Allen had rubbed some people the wrong way and it would be easier to talk to those who had liked him and Lola. "Yes. I'm here visiting her for a few days. I've gotten to know Amy Sanders. She told me she had come to town to see her parents and that they had a trailer over there." I pointed across the street.

Grace frowned. "Yes, I have met Amy, too." She stepped away from me toward the house. "I need to go in now."

"Wait, I just wanted to ask you…" but Grace had dropped her rose clippers and gone inside. They would rust quickly if they laid on the grass for long. I slipped through the gate in the hedge and put the clippers on the porch.

That was odd. She had almost run away from me. Oh, well. I would try somebody else. Who next? Amy's list said that Mavis O'Reilly ran a shop where she sold her ceramics, so she should be there. I would try talking to her.

This time I decided I would start off by telling her what I wanted. Maybe I would get some better information if I caught her off guard.

Mavis had remodeled the front of a small beach house into a ceramics shop. Mavis' Muds, the sign by the door read. Mavis sounded like she had a sense of humor, anyway. A tiny bell tinkled as I opened the door to Mavis' shop and I almost forgot my errand. She had done things with clay and glass that I would never have imagined. Tall, slender vases soared on high shelves, plates of fused glass glowed like gems on lower glass shelves in front of the windows, and every other sort of dish, cup, and wall ornament hung everywhere. This would be no place for Henry with his busy paws and waving tail, that was for sure. I chose gifts for several people and took them to the counter. A woman came out from the back area where I could see a kiln and potter's wheel.

"May I help you?"

"Yes," I said, "I found some treasures. Did you do all this?"

She nodded. "Yes, I'm Mavis O'Reilly and this is my shop."

"You do amazing work," I said. "I have done a little leaded stained glass in the past and always wanted to do glass fusing with the leftovers."

"That's how I got into it, too. One of the things I learned the hard way is that in order for the glass pieces to fuse they must be made by the same manufacturer. They need to become liquid all at the same time, otherwise when the pieces cool they just fall apart and glass made by different companies has different melting points. I use bull's eye glass almost exclusively."

Mavis took me into her work area and showed me some of the forms and things she used to make her fused and slumped glass objects. I wondered how she had achieved the free-form edges of her vases.

"You just set the piece of glass over the form," she said, "Then watch through the holes in the side of the kiln until it has almost slumped enough. Then you turn off the heat and let it cool. The glass will continue to slump and sag until it has started to cool. You never know exactly what you are going to get until the kiln has cooled off enough so you can safely open it. Open it too soon, and the glass will shatter."

"This is amazing, Mavis. Thank you so much for showing me all this. I better pay you for my things and get out of your way."

While she rang up my bill I said, "Do you know anything about what happened to the Armstrongs, the couple that had the place across the street? Amy is a friend of mine and I told her I would help her find her parents."

Mavis fumbled with the bread plate I had selected for Georgia, my best buddy back home, and nearly dropped it. "No," she said. "I really don't have time to pay much attention to what goes on outside."

"So you didn't see when the trailer was moved out or anything?"

"No, not really. Here's your things. That'll be $84.10." I handed her my VISA card and she turned to run it through the machine. "Did you happen to see the Armstrongs leave?"

She handed me the receipt to sign, shaking her head and keeping her face turned away from me. "Like I said, I don't pay much attention to what's going on outside. Now, if you don't want to buy anything else, I have some clay on the wheel I need to get back to. Thank you. Good-bye." Mavis disappeared behind a curtain in the back of her shop. The eager-to-show-off-her-skills artist was gone. There was nothing else for me to do but leave.

I went and sat in the Blazer to think. I was zero for two so far. But, even though nobody had talked to me, I had learned something anyway. For some reason, the very mention of the Armstrong name evoked fear. Now I really wanted to know what had happened to them. I looked at my watch. Maybe I had time for one more visit before I would be intruding on anybody's dinner time.

CHAPTER 15

▼

I could see someone puttering around in the back yard of the house with a big garden. He was wearing bib overalls and had on a straw hat. This must be Frank Ottman's place.

"That's quite a garden you have there," I called to him over the fence.

"It does look pretty good, doesn't it. Here, have a tomato," he said, setting down his hoe. "I'm Frank Ottman, who might you be?"

This looked like someone who could have been a crony of Allen's. I would try that connection first. "I'm Maggie Jackson, Allen Bowen's niece. I'm here visiting my aunt Lola."

"Well, how do you do? Allen was a good fishing buddy of mine and I still miss him. You want to come in and take a load off?" He held the gate open for me.

We walked over to the porch and he offered me a chair. "Lemonade?"

"I would love some," I said.

"So how is Lola doing?" Frank said as he poured. "I haven't gotten over to see her in a while."

"She's doing fine, still painting her pictures. She misses the people she used to see all the time at the Beach House, but she's also glad not to have all the hard work."

"Yeah, I can imagine. That diner is a going place. What brings you to town?"

"There's a quilting seminar going on at the Seacoast Inn and I came over to teach a couple of classes. I have a small quilting business in Spokane and it seemed like a good chance to visit Lola and get some rest.

"I wondered, though, if you could help me with something. I met Amy Sanders, George and Bethel Armstrong's daughter, working at the Beach House Lola used to own. She said that you were friends with them and that you might know what happened to them."

Frank frowned. "I told Amy everything I knew, which wasn't much. George and Bethel were here one day then the next day they were gone."

"That's what Amy told me. But her parents had invited her to come stay with them; they even sent her a plane ticket. She can't imagine that they would just take off without telling her."

Frank looked distinctly uncomfortable now, frowning and moving about restlessly in his chair. I got the feeling the only reason he hadn't run off like Grace or cut off talking to me like Mavis was because he had been such a good friend of Allen's. Besides, I was sitting on his porch with a glass of lemonade in my hand. He looked around, as if making sure there was nobody nearby. He said, "Sheriff Krupe came around the day after Amy was here. He said that she was a trouble-maker and that it would 'be in my best interests,' as he put it, to forget that I ever knew the Armstrongs."

"Why would he do that?" I asked.

Frank was sweating now and I thought he almost looked scared. "I don't know," he said, fanning his face with his hat. "I just know that Ollie Krupe is not, shall we say, the straightest arrow in the quiver."

I sat for a minute and thought. It would not surprise me at all if Oliver Krupe was dishonest, or on the take, or something. His whole attitude with Amy had been so unprofessional and bordered on incompetence. "So, you think he's crooked?"

Frank looked around again. "You better go. I don't want Ollie to know that you were talking to me about any of this. I don't want any trouble."

"But, you think…"

Frank waved his hand in front of my face, cutting me off. "If I should happen to hear from the Armstrongs, I will let you know. I know Lola's number. It's been nice talking to you." He stood up. It was obvious that my visit was over.

I walked out of Frank's yard and stood by the road for a minute. What to do next? The blue house on Amy's list that must be where the sisters live was dark, but there were lights on at the house I assumed was the Medcaff's—I could see stables in the back. But, I could also see a man sitting at a table in what must be a breakfast nook in the kitchen while a woman moved back and forth, carrying dishes. I decided to wait until the next day to talk to them, rather than interrupt their meal. I headed back to Lola's.

CHAPTER 16

▼

Lola was outside pulling the dead blooms off her marigolds.

"You look troubled," she said. "What's going on?"

"Rick always says he can tell what I'm thinking just by my expression and it looks like you can, too. I'd make a lousy poker player. You are right, though. I am worried. I went out to where Amy's parents had bought that lot and put in their trailer and tried to talk to the neighbors. A couple of them practically ran away when I told them what I wanted and only Frank Ottman was willing to talk to me, and him not much."

"I know Frank," said Lola, "He and Allen used to do a lot of fishing."

"Yeah, that's what he said and I think that is the only reason he would talk to me at all. Something is definitely off about the Armstrongs leaving the way they did, but the way he talked that Sheriff Krupe has warned everybody not to say anything about it."

"I'm done here," said Lola. Let's go in and get some coffee." She frowned as she sat down at her kitchen table. "There has been something off about Oliver Krupe ever since he took office. Mike Thompson had been our sheriff previously. He was a great guy and it was a real tragedy when he drowned in a fishing accident. Oliver had been hired as a part-time deputy, but he somehow managed to schmooze his way into being appointed to finish out Mike's term. Then, he put on a pretty aggressive election campaign and was elected to a second term. People are sorry about that now, but we really can't do much until the next election. Nobody really likes him, and we also don't trust him. There have been some funny stories go around, but nothing anybody could substantiate."

"That doesn't surprise me a bit, Lola," I said. "He was so totally unconcerned about Amy getting attacked, in fact, he refuses to believe it was anything but an accident. He seemed angry at her for being hurt and then at me for finding her. He wouldn't even call for help. But I don't know why he would act that way. It wasn't like he had to drive her to the hospital himself. It makes me wonder what he really knows about Amy's parents disappearing."

"Oh, Maggie, be careful," said Lola, wringing her hands, "If Oliver Krupe thinks you are interfering with him it could be dangerous."

"You're scared of him, too, aren't you?"

Lola just nodded, looking miserable. "He can really make life difficult for people that cross him. I just try to stay away from him."

"Is there anybody in Long Beach or Ocean Park who could help us?"

"Not really," she said. "Oliver is the sheriff for the whole peninsula; his office is in Ocean Side because he liked that impressive building—he feels it exemplifies the office, or some such tripe—and he was able to convince the people to agree with him and finance moving the office there. It had been in a free-standing building that was closer to Long Beach than the current office is."

"Well, this is crazy. I'm going to find Amy's parents and if this is a crooked cop he'll be sorry!"

Brave words, idiot, I thought. Just how do you propose to do all this in the week and a half you have left here? And how to accomplish it without putting Lola in danger? Well, I had the will; I would find the way.

I left Lola sitting at the table, staring off into space. I wanted to find out about Oliver Krupe, but after what Lola said I knew that nobody in Ocean Side or probably anywhere else on this end of the peninsula would be willing to talk to me about him. I went into Lola's den and sat down at her phone desk. I picked up the receiver, but the minute I heard the steady buzz of the dial tone I hung up. Paranoia was setting in and I decided it might be best not to use her phone for this call.

"I'm going to Jack's to make a call," I told Lola, "I'll be back in a few minutes. Need anything from the store?"

She just shook her head.

The phone booth was around on the side of the building near the garbage cans. I should have some privacy.

"Hello?"

"Hi, Sully, it's Maggie. I'm so glad you are there." Sully is my shotgun-toting, whiskey-swilling neighbor. She is almost a caricature of the crusty old lady with a heart of gold. She was helping Rick keep Cleo and Marmalade, the little lady cats, and Brandy, the big brindle greyhound, fed and happy while I was gone. Sully was taking the mail in every day, too. I knew she liked my big TV and selection of DVD movies and I had told her to make herself at home. I wasn't surprised to find her there.

"Hey, Mag, how'd the classes go?"

"Really well. It was a fun group and I think they learned a lot. Would you do something for me, please?"

"Sure, kid, what's up?"

"Grab a piece of paper and write down the name Oliver Krupe, that's K R U P E. When you have a minute tomorrow, would you see if you can reach Martin Adams at the Sheriff's office and give him that name? I need to know if Marty knows this Krupe guy."

"Got it. You want me to have him call you?"

Sully loved intrigue and knowing what was going on. She would delight in being a go-between, that I knew.

"No, I don't really want anybody around here to know what I am doing. Tell him I'm check with him day after tomorrow and see if he has had time to learn anything. I think he has my email address, if he doesn't it's on my business cards and there's a box of them in my office next to my computer monitor. Please give him the address when you talk to him."

"Will do," said Sully. "You find more druggies? I'da thought you'da had your fill of criminals after that last time."

"No, nothing that exciting. But, Marty is the only cop I really know and I hope he can help me. I don't want to say much right now, but I will let you know what is going on as soon as I can."

"Rick's not gonna like this, so I won't tell him," said Sully.

I heard her distinctive cackle. "Thanks Sully, and thanks for babysitting. I'll see you in a week or so."

Lola was just finishing dishing up a lovely smelling beef stew and I could see a plate of fluffy biscuits waiting on the table. I'd have to careful or by the end of next week none of my clothes would fit.

"That smells wonderful, Lola. Where is Amy, by the way?"

"She's in the bathroom. She napped most of the afternoon and talked about going back to her rented room tonight, but I convinced her to stay here one more night," Lola said.

"And the aroma of that roast beef stew sure helped convince me," said Amy, as she sat down at the table.

"You look like you feel a lot better," I said. "Your bruise is even starting to fade."

She reached up and carefully touched her head. "Yes, I do feel more like myself and that spot isn't nearly as sore. Did you find out anything today, Maggie?"

"Well, mostly that everybody is afraid of Olive Krupe and also scared to talk about your parents." Henry had crawled up into my lap and I had to keep pushing aside his waving tail so I could see. He wasn't used to being left behind and now he wanted attention. I stroked his sleek black back and he purred like a running chain saw. "Just a minute, kitty, and I'll get you something to eat, too."

"Did anybody have anything helpful to tell you?" Amy's face was pale and tears stood in her eyes.

"Not really," I said, "But I am going to go nose around again some more tomorrow."

The stew was wonderful and we all stuffed ourselves. We had just settled down to watch a movie when there was a banging on the front door. I got up to answer it.

I could see the uniform, but this was not Sheriff Krupe. This person was thinner, and taller with neatly combed hair and sharply creased uniform pants. I opened the door.

"Maggie Jackson?" he asked. At my nod he said, "I have been sent over by the sheriff to tell you to stop harassing the citizens about the supposed disappearance of George and Bethel Armstrong. We know that these people moved away by their own decision and that is to be the end of it."

I looked at him for a minute. "What is your name, please?"

"Oh, sorry," he said, color flooding his face. "I'm Deputy Glen Gunnison with the Pacific County Sheriff's office." He drew himself up taller, pride evident in his face.

"Well, Deputy Gunnison, I was not harassing people, as you put it. Amy Sanders, the daughter of George and Bethel Armstrong, asked me if I would help her. She was invited by her parents to come and visit them, they even sent her a plane ticket, but when she arrived they were nowhere to be found. All I did was stop by the neighbors around the Armstrong's place and ask a couple of questions. It does not make sense to me that anybody would invite their daughter to visit and then just move away and not tell her. I am going to continue to try to find out what happened to Amy's parents and you can tell that Oliver Krupe who sent you here to go jump in the bay."

Glen stared at me. "What do you mean, they sent a plane ticket?"

Now it was my turn to be embarrassed. Obviously, Glen Gunnison was not wholly in the loop on this. "Let's sit down out here on the porch," I said, "And you can tell me if this sounds as funny to you as it does to me."

I went over Amy's story one more time, then asked him if he knew about her being attacked.

"No," he said, looking shocked. "When did that happen?"

"Day before yesterday," I said. "I was walking on the beach with my cat when we found her. It was obvious she had been hit on the head."

"Why didn't you make a report?" the deputy asked me, frowning.

"I tried, Deputy Gunnison, but your boss said that it was just an accident and practically threw me out of the office."

"Please call me Glen," he said, "This is just a small place." He shook his head. "That sounds like Oliver, for sure. He doesn't want anything to be wrong in his little part of the world."

"I don't get it, though, Glen. I can't blame him for wanting things to be wonderful all the time, but he wouldn't even consider filing a missing persons report for Amy about her parents, even with the plane ticket and their invitation to her to visit and everything."

Glen stood up. "I need to get going. There really isn't much I can do to help without going behind Oliver's back and I need my job. Try to keep a low profile, though, Maggie, if you continue to try and help Amy. You don't want Sheriff Krupe angry at you." He got in his car and drove away.

I watched his car until the taillights disappeared around the corner at the end of the street. Glen Gunnison had been sent over by Oliver Krupe, that was obvious. If Oliver was willing to go to such lengths to stop any inquiry about Amy's parents, then there must be something to it. Now I was really determined to find out what was going on.

"Who was that at the door, Maggie?" Lola asked as I walked back to where she and Amy were sitting.

"Deputy Glen Gunnison, sent here by Krupe to warn me off asking about the Armstrongs," I said.

Lola shook her head. "I'm not surprised. Oliver expects to get his own way all the time. What did you tell Glen?"

"I told him Amy's whole story; there was a lot he didn't know. At first I thought maybe he was going to look into things, but really all he did was tell me to be careful not to upset Oliver. It doesn't sound like he will be a lot of help. He did say I didn't want Oliver Krupe mad at me."

"Well, he's right, Maggie. You are going to have to be careful."

"Oh, Maggie, let's just drop it," said Amy. "I don't want anybody else to get hurt." She reached up and rubbed the bump on her head.

"No way am I stopping now," I said. "That would mean that Oliver Krupe wins. I think he is somehow involved in your parents' disappearance and I'm going to find out how. Maybe I can convince this deputy to help me, too."

Brave words, indeed, but would I be able to actually do anything? Amy looked at me with adoration; Lola looked worried.

CHAPTER 17

▼

The next day Henry and I took another walk on the beach. I had not slept well, my brain was spinning all night trying to think of how I was going to help Amy, if nobody would talk to me. I looked at my watch. It was still early, but I was going to go talk to the Medcaffs today and Oliver Krupe be damned!

Lola was pulling her car into the driveway as Henry and I got back from our walk. "I just took Amy back to her boarding house," she said. "I hope she is going to be okay. She was going to go and see if she still had her job at Lucille's, too." Lola did not look happy.

"I'm going to go and try to talk to the Medcaffs. They are the only neighbors of the Armstrongs I didn't get to yesterday," I said. "If you hear from Amy tell her I hope to have some news for her."

I went in to my room to change. Henry sat and looked at me, head tipped to one side and eyes alert. He was hoping for another adventure.

"I'm sorry, Henry, but you have to stay home again. As soon as I can we'll go out for another walk."

Henry curled up on my bed turned his head away from me, looking mad. I knew better than to assume he could actually understand me, but it sure seemed that he did. I rubbed his ears and scratched his chin, but he would not purr. I pulled off my beach-walking clothes and took out my favorite jeans as a test. If I had to lie down to zip them up then I was getting too much of Lola's good cooking. Good. The zipper went up while I was standing. I tied a sweatshirt around my waist. Even though it was summer the weather could get chilly in a hurry near the ocean. I left Henry sulking on the bed and went out and got into the Blazer.

"Hi, Eve? I'm Maggie Jackson, could I talk to you for a minute?"

"Sure," said the young woman, holding a fluffy dog back with her leg, "As long as you aren't selling anything!" Her smile was warm and she opened the door to let me in.

We sat down in a cozy room with quilts over the backs of all the chairs and the sofa. The dog, a poodle mix of some sort, came over and leaned against my knee, begging to be pet. While I scratched its ears I looked around.

"These are lovely quilts," I said, "Did you make them?"

She ducked her head and blushed. "Yeah, but I'm just starting out and they aren't too good. I don't know how to properly put colors together."

"Well, do you like them?" I asked her. At her nod I went on, "Then that's all that matters. I have a quilting studio back in Spokane where I live and I teach beginning quilting classes. One of the first things I tell people is that the only real rule for quilting is even, quarter-inch seams. The choice of pattern and color combinations is everybody's own choice. If you like pink and brown together, then you should make your quilt pink and brown."

Eve chuckled. "Oh, that's great to hear. Now maybe I'll be brave enough to make that purple and green combo I can see in my head. But, I have a feeling you didn't come to talk about my quilts, did you?"

"No, I didn't. I'm here in town visiting my aunt, Lola Bowen. She used to own Lucille's Beach House. I got to know the waitress there, Amy Sanders, and she asked me to help her find out what happened to her parents, who used to live across the street over there."

Eve leaned forward, her eyes eager. "I would like to know what happened to them, too. One night I heard some noises over there and the next day the Armstrongs were gone."

"What, completely gone, trailer and all?"

"No, just them. I used to see Bethel every morning and sometimes we would have coffee together. With Dick working with the horses all day it gets kind of lonely here. I would go over and visit with Bethel occasionally when George was puttering in his shop and we went shopping together a few times. I really liked her."

"Had Bethel told you anything about being unhappy living here or about going back east?"

"No, not at all. She said they used to live in Chicago, in a downtown apartment, and she was really enjoying being out and away from all the hustle and bustle of a big city. She told me she was going to try and get her daughter to move out here, too. She said her daughter, it's Amy isn't it? was coming to visit. Bethel even sent her a plane ticket."

This woman was a fountain of information and willing to share. I hoped she would have something really helpful to say.

"On the night before they disappeared did anything funny or odd happen?"

She sat and thought for a minute. "No, not really. Carl was over there helping George fix his TV antenna, but he was over at their place all the time."

"Who's Carl?"

"Carl Rolley, he's the son of the people that own Lucille's Beach House. I never liked him much, but Bethel said he helped them out a lot."

"Who's this? What's going on here, Eve?"

Eve jumped, her hand at her throat. A man had come silently into the room, tricky with the cowboy boots he was wearing. He pulled off his Stetson and glowered at me. I caught the faint, but pleasant, aroma of horses coming off his clothes.

"Dick, good heavens, you scared me to death. This is Maggie, what was your last name again?"

"I'm Maggie Jackson."

"What are you doing here?" Dick asked, leaning over me, his fists clenched at his sides. I looked at Eve, her face was white and she was moving her head back and forth in tiny motions. She looked terrified.

"My aunt, Lola Bowen, lives here in Ocean Side. I have a quilt studio in Spokane and I came to stay with Lola and attend a quilting conference at the Seacoast Inn."

"You remember, Dick. Susan said she was going to go to that. I wanted to go, too, Maggie, but Dick needed me to help him with the horses over the weekend." Eve's voice trembled.

"Shut up, Eve, I'm not talking to you. What are you doing in my house, bothering my wife?"

I smiled, pretending not to notice his rudeness or his aggressive stance. "I talked to several ladies who live in the area and they told me Eve made wonderful quilts. I just stopped by on the chance that she would have time to show them to me. She really does beautiful work." I patted the quilt I was sitting on that covered the sofa.

"How do I know you aren't lying to me?" he said, his frown unchanged.

"Dick! Don't be rude! She just…"

He whirled back to face his wife. "I thought I told you to shut up. Now get out in the kitchen and make me some coffee. I'll deal with this."

This man was a brute. I could easily imagine him beating his wife for "disobeying" him. I wanted to do everything I could to make sure that did not happen.

Ignoring the fuming man, I talked to Eve's back as she went into the kitchen for the coffee her husband had ordered her to make.

"I need to get going, Eve. Thank you for showing me your quilts—they are lovely. Here's my card. If you ever get to Spokane come and see me. I'll show you my longarm machine that we were talking about and you can give it a whirl. It was nice to meet you, too, Mr. Medcaff."

I stood up and set my card on the coffee table. "I can see myself out," I said, heading for the door. As I opened it I glanced back. Dick had picked up my card and was studying it. Thanks goodness I had brought some with me. I hoped this would be good enough to spare Eve any trouble. But, I still wanted to talk to her. She would have more to say, I was sure. I would try calling her the next day; maybe we could meet somewhere.

CHAPTER 18

▼

I pulled the Blazer into Lola's driveway and sat for a minute, exhausted. So much for a relaxing time away from home and work responsibilities. I was ready for another of Lola's great meals and hopefully a good night's sleep.

"Maggie! Thank heavens you're back," said Lola, dashing out her front door with her cordless phone in her hand. "Amy just called a few minutes ago. She went back to her boarding house this afternoon and she just called to say that somebody had broken into her room and torn everything up. She said the landlady has kicked her out, too. She sounded hysterical and I was just going over there to get her. Would you drive?"

There goes my peaceful evening, I thought. "Sure," I said, "Hop in."

Amy was sitting in the middle of her bed, tears running down her face. A large, fat women in a wrinkled muumuu stood in the doorway, glaring at her. Pink foam curlers bobbed in her hair as she talked.

"...and you have about fifteen seconds to get your stuff and get out of here. I've had enough trouble from the likes of you, you troublesome little bitch."

"Why, Audrey Holt, what a fine way for you to talk. What would the other guild members think?"

"Oh, Lola, where did you come from?" The woman turned, a phony smile pasted across her face.

"I came to get Amy, if it's any of your business."

I had never seen Lola really angry before and it was something to behold. Her normally tidy bun had come partway unraveled and tendrils of hair whipped around her face like Medusa's snakes. Her eyes flashed fire.

Audrey stepped back, looking startled. "Well, she is trouble," she said, pointing at Amy. "Ever since she got here I've had the sheriff at my door, the phone ringing at all hours of the day and night, and all other sorts of upset. I'm glad to kick her out of my house; maybe now she'll go back where she belongs."

"She came to town looking for her parents, who are missing, Audrey. I had thought you were a caring, Christian woman, but now I wonder. Come on, Amy, let's get you out of this place."

While Lola chewed out Audrey, I looked around. The room was a mess. All of Amy's clothes had been taken out of the closet and thrown on the floor. The bureau drawers had been pulled out and dumped, and there was trash, looked like from a kitchen garbage bag, tossed over everything. The room stunk. The bed had been stripped and the sheets were stuffed into the window.

"Get out of my way, Audrey. Go get me a plastic bag," said Lola, as she started to pick things up. "Amy, where is your suitcase?"

Within minutes Lola had gathered up all Amy's soiled clothes and put them in the bag Audrey brought for her. She pulled the bedding out of the open window and dumped it at Audrey's feet. I put the few items that were still clean into the suitcase and helped Amy get the rest of her things out of the bathroom down the hall. Luckily, this room had been spared the wrath of the vandal. We loaded everything into the Blazer.

It was a warm day, but Amy was shivering in the back seat. I wrapped her in the quilt I keep in the back and we headed to Lola's.

"Here, drink this," said Lola, handing Amy a mug of steaming cocoa. "It'll warm your blood."

"Then tell us what happened," I said.

Amy sipped for a minute in silence and I was glad to see some color return to her pale face. She set her cup down with a sigh, tears again brimming in her eyes.

"Nothing really *happened*. I just went up to my room and found the door open. You saw the mess; I couldn't think what to do, so I just called your aunt. I hope that was okay, Lola?"

"Of course it was," said Lola, patting Amy's shoulder. "I'm glad you did."

"My question is who would do this?" I said. "Could you tell if anything was stolen, Amy?"

"No, my camera and laptop computer were still there; those are the only two really valuable things I have. What little cash I have, about $25, and my debit card were in my purse and I had that with me. Besides, why would a thief dump garbage all over? Does somebody hate me?"

That thought had occurred to me, but I hadn't want to scare Amy by mentioning it. She wasn't dumb, though, she had picked that up on her own. This looked to me more like a threat of some kind, rather than a simple burglary. Somebody wanted Amy to leave Ocean Side. Now my suspicions about her parents' disappearance had solidified into a feeling of certainty.

"What I am going to do now?" Amy said, dropping her head onto her crossed arms. "I have nowhere to go."

"Yes you do," said Lola, "In fact, you're already there. You can stay here as long as you need to."

"But I can't pay..." Amy started to say.

"Don't be ridiculous!" Lola looked insulted. "There is no way I would expect you to pay me. Lots of people helped me out in the past, now it's my turn."

"Well, I will help you with the housework and the cooking anyway," Amy said. "I actually like that kind of work, anyway."

"Oh, all right," said Lola. "I suppose that's fair. But, you need to use your time finding out about your parents. I'm afraid something has happened to them."

Oh, boy, I thought, that's done it. Amy is going to fall apart. She is already so fragile and to hear that might just finish her off. Amy surprised me, though. She nodded her head eagerly. "Yes, I think so too. But I need to know, Maggie, did you find out anything today?"

"Not a lot, Amy, except that Eve Medcaff is married to a real nasty guy. I got the feeling she has some information for me, but he wouldn't let her talk to me. I'm going to try and call her tomorrow." I was going to go back and talk to Audrey at the house where Amy had been living, too. Hopefully she would be interested in finding out who had broken into her house.

CHAPTER 19

▼

After a night spent tossing and turning, my brain churning with all that was going on, I sat out on the patio in the morning sunshine with my coffee, trying to come up with a game plan. I was going to try and talk to Audrey, but I also wanted to try getting in touch with Eve. I would call Marty Adams in Spokane too, and see if he knew anything about Oliver Krupe. I watched the ocean for a minute. I would go see Audrey first.

Henry had spent the day before scattering as many of Lola's things as he could carry around her house. He was upset, being left behind, so I decided to take him with me. He could be a real ice-breaker and I might need that at Audrey's. I put his harness on him and he hopped into his carrier when I brought it out; he was eager to travel.

At Audrey's house I let Henry out. He poked around on her porch while I waited for her to answer the door. I had been thinking about how to approach her and I hoped my plan would work.

"Hi, Audrey," I said, ignoring her frown. "I wonder if I can talk to you for a minute?"

She looked out the door and saw Henry. For an instant her face softened, maybe she liked cats.

"What do you want?"

"Well, I wanted to thank you for helping my aunt and me with your boarder yesterday. It must have been quite a job, cleaning up that mess. I was hoping to help you find out who did it. May I come in real quick?" I tried not to gag, she had been about as helpful the day before as a rubber crutch.

"That is a beautiful cat," she said. "I can't believe he lets you put that harness on him." She watched Henry nose around for a minute. He came over and put his paws on the bottom of the screen door, then reached up for the handle. "Oh, he wants to come in." She frowned at me again. "I suppose you can bring him in, although I don't know anything about who broke in here yesterday."

Inside the house I unfastened Henry's leash. He glanced around the room, then walked over to where Audrey sat. He jumped up into her lap and gazed into her face. Then he oozed his body up her chest until his paws were resting on her shoulder. Before I could warn her, he started to lick her ear.

"Oooo, that tickles, kitty." Audrey was laughing and stroking his back. I couldn't hear him, but I knew he was purring. "He really likes me, doesn't he?"

"He sure does!" I said, not bothering to tell her that he liked most everybody and was obsessed with licking peoples' ears. "He'll do that forever unless you make him stop."

Audrey pulled Henry down into her lap where he promptly curled up and continued to gaze adoringly at her. What a soft-soap artist he was. It was like he knew I needed her to be happy so that she would talk to me.

"So, do you have any idea what happened yesterday?" I asked.

Audrey looked up at me, a smile on her face. "This is a great cat," she said, then she frowned, looking puzzled. "No, I really don't know anything. I was gone to the store and when I came home I found Amy sitting in the middle of that mess."

"Did you notice anybody hanging around before you left or did you get any funny phone calls yesterday?"

"No, I didn't see anybody around, but now that you mention it, I had two phone calls yesterday where there was nobody there when I answered, but I didn't think too much about that. I seem to get lots of hang-ups, probably just wrong numbers."

"Has anybody else called you since then?"

She sat and thought for a minute, her hand continuing to stroke Henry, who had gone to sleep. "I don't think so, why?"

"May I try something? Where is your phone?"

Audrey pointed to a table by the door. I picked up her cordless phone and brought it back to where I was sitting. I hoped the phone company here had that last call return service. I crossed my fingers and punched the *69 code. After a second I heard that odd computer voice telling me that the number of the last call had been 555 6752.

I read the number out loud. "Is that number familiar to you?" I asked Audrey.

"No. Why, is that the number of the person that called me yesterday and hung up?"

"It could be, assuming that nobody else has tried to call you and you didn't hear the phone."

She shook her head. "No, I don't think so. I haven't been anywhere since then and I can even hear the phone ring when I'm in the shower."

"Well, that will be a place to start, if I can figure out whose number this is," I said. "Did you have any company yesterday, someone you weren't expecting?"

"No, not really. Carl Rolley was going to come do some yard work for me today, but he came by yesterday afternoon instead and started working. He told me his other job had finished sooner than he expected. That's him right there, running the weed whacker out in the back." Audrey pointed out a dining room window. There was an alley behind her house and a tall, thin man with an unkempt head of red hair was chopping down the weeds growing there. An aged blue Ford Galaxy was parked in the alley.

"Is that his car?" I asked.

"Yes, it is. You don't suspect Carl of anything, do you? He has always been a perfect gentleman and a great help to me since my husband died." Audrey was glaring at me again.

"No, not a bit," I said. "I just wondered if that were his car. Thank you so much for all your help." Henry woke up and stretched. He could tell it was time to go. "If it's all right with you, I think I'll just go ask Carl if he saw anything yesterday. He could have seen something if he was working here when your house was broken into."

Audrey had relaxed again. "Oh, you're welcome and I'm sorry I wasn't more help. Yes, that's fine, go talk to Carl. I would like to know who got in here, too."

I clipped Henry's leash onto his harness and kept him close to me. I wasn't sure this man would be as happy to see him as Audrey had been.

"What's with the damn cat?" he said, shutting off the weed whacker when he saw us approaching.

"Oh, he just likes to walk on a leash. Are you Carl Rolley?"

"Yeah," he said, "Who's asking?"

I looked down at Henry. He had stopped nosing around in the weeds and was watching Carl. A narrow band of fur stood up the length of his back and his eyes were dilated. He was not a fan of Carl's, that was for sure. "My name is Maggie

Jackson, my aunt is Lola Bowen and I am here visiting her. I met Amy Sanders a couple of days ago. You might know who she is; she was staying here at Audrey's. Yesterday afternoon somebody broke into Audrey's house and went to Amy's room and trashed the place. I told Audrey I would ask around and see if anybody knows anything; she would like to know who was in her house."

Was that a fleeting smirk I saw on his face, or was I just looking for something? I waited for him to answer. Henry was a black statue at my feet, staring at Carl.

"What makes you think I know anything?" he said, the smirk now obvious.

I flipped my hands out to the sides, trying to look a little foolish and as non-threatening as possible. "Well, you look like an observant, intelligent, kind of guy. Audrey said you were here doing yard work and I told her I'd ask you if you saw anything. Did you see a strange car or anybody around?" Rick would be hooting by now. He knew I wasn't the kissy-face, butter- 'em-up sort, but I felt that was the best approach to use with this Carl Rolley character.

He frowned, trying to convince me of his concern, I thought. "Yes, as a matter of fact I did see a dark blue minivan that I've never seen around here before. There was a blond lady driving it."

That was too glib, I thought. If there was a blond in a van around yesterday I was Hillary Clinton.

"Thank you so much," I gushed. "I'll go tell Audrey that, maybe she will know who it was. Thanks for all your help."

Carl pulled himself up taller and puffed out his bony chest. "No problem," he said.

Henry pulled his lips back in a silent grimace. I had to tug a couple of times on his leash to get him to move. Carl was so intent on looking important that he didn't even notice all the cat teeth.

I tapped on Audrey's back door. "Carl says he saw a blond lady in a blue mini van around here yesterday. Does that ring any bells for you?" She shook her head. "Well, if you think of anything, give Lola a call, will you?"

She gave Henry a fond look. "Okay."

Back in the Blazer, Henry's fur had smoothed out. "You didn't like that guy much, did you, fella?" His only reply was a yellow-eyed squint.

Now what? I decided to go back down to Jack's and use the public phone again. I would give both Marty Adams and Eve a call. I would start with Eve.

"Hello, Eve? This is Maggie Jackson, I came to see you yesterday. I hope everything was okay with your husband after I left."

"Yes," she said, "I do remember requesting that book."

Huh? "Do you know who this is?" I asked.

"Yes, that's right," she said.

I gave myself a swift kick, of course, her husband was right there. "Is Dick close enough where he can hear you?"

"Yes."

"Well, I wondered if I could talk to you again, maybe meet someplace?"

"Just a minute." Her voice became softer, like she had taken the receiver away from her mouth. "Dick?" I heard her say, "Would it be okay for me to run down to the library this afternoon? I had asked them to call me when the cookbook was returned that has that cheese bread recipe you want to me make. They said the book is back and that they are holding it for me."

I could hear Dick's voice in the background, but I couldn't make out his words. "Okay," I heard Eve say. "I'll go about two and it shouldn't take me more than an hour." Her voice was loud in my ear again. "Thank you for calling. I'll be in later to make a copy of that recipe."

"Good job, Eve," I said. "I'll find the cookbook section in the library and see you there at two o'clock today."

She hung up without replying. Now I would just need to find out where the library was located. But first, I dropped some more coins into the phone then dialed the 555 6792 number I had gotten from Audrey's phone. I let the phone ring on, but after fifteen rings I hung up. Nobody answering and no voice mail response to give me a clue, either. I'd have to figure out whose number this was some other way.

I looked at my watch. It was just barely noon. I had lots of time to try to catch Marty at work and then go back to Lola's and see if I could figure out who had called Audrey's yesterday and hung up without talking. I punched in my calling card number and the Spokane Sheriff's Office number.

"Maggie!" Marty's voice boomed through the phone at me. "Don't tell me you are tangled up in another drug mess!" I could hear him laughing.

"No, not this time. I am wondering about some things, though. You got the name of the sheriff I sent you?"

"Yes," he said, his voice serious now, "And I'm a little bit concerned. I know Oliver Krupe from my academy days. He was just barely able to squeak through both the physical and classroom parts of the program. Then he got a job as a deputy in one of the small towns around Spokane—I can't remember which one right now. He didn't last long, though. There were questions about his professional conduct and his inappropriate use of force. He was on the verge of being fired when he quit. He sort of dropped out of sight and I haven't heard much about him since. Why are you asking about him?"

"Well, to make a long story short, I'm visiting my aunt Lola in Ocean Side and he is the sheriff here. I met a young woman who is trying to find out what happened to her parents. They had moved here and invited her to come visit, but when she arrived they were gone. Oliver Krupe has refused to help her in any way and would not even let her file a missing persons report. She recently sustained a head injury and the doctor said the injuries were inflicted on her and not from a fall. This Krupe character won't even look into it, insisting it was an accident. I'm the lucky one who found her lying unconscious on the beach and he would not even call EMS."

Marty sighed. "That sounds like Ollie, all right. He's not a very good cop, but he thinks he's something special. Have you ever read any of Ed McBain's 86th Precinct police procedural novels?"

"Yes, I have, but what does that have to do with anything?"

"Well," said Marty, "Remember the Oliver Weeks character, the one who thinks he is such a fabulous cop and is also convinced that he looks like W. C. Fields? McBain has Weeks talking like he's Fields and it drives detective Steve Carella crazy. The cops call him Fat Ollie."

I did know what Marty was talking about. Oliver Weeks' physical description was something like Oliver Krupe's, now that I thought about it. And while Oliver Weeks was not a stupendous cop, he was sexist and a bigot besides, he was an adequate policeman. He even saved Steve Carella's life once.

"Oliver Krupe considers himself to be the personification of Oliver Weeks because they share a first name and body type, I suppose. If you ever see him in a social situation he'll pull that W. C. Fields stuff, too. But, that's just him being stupid. I wouldn't trust him, in fact, I'd beware of him. He is not above using force and intimidation to get what he wants," Marty said.

"Great. That's all I need, a bad cop. Thanks for the info, Marty. Now I have another request, but I don't know if you can help me or not. These people that disappeared came in a trailer towed by a pickup with a small car hitched to the trailer. Is there any way you could find out what happened to the car or the truck, or both? The car is a 1996 red Chevrolet GEO Metro LSI, and the truck a blue Chevy. The truck is a fairly new one, too, a '99, I think. Amy's stepfather had a thing for Chevrolets, it seems. That's all Amy knows, she didn't even have the license number for either vehicle. Her parents' names are George and Bethel Armstrong and I would assume the car is still licensed in Illinois, Chicago to be exact. That is where they moved from and they hadn't been here very long."

"I'll see what I can do, but it might be tough, Maggie. I might be able to find out if they changed either of the registrations to Washington state."

"Thanks, Marty. If we know who has the car now maybe we can figure out where these people are. Too bad Henry can't pull out a piece of relevant paperwork out of a crack in the wall like he found that baggie of cocaine at the clinic."

"You be careful, Maggie. Just because Henry helped you escape Linda Mancusco's clutches doesn't mean he can do that again."

"I will be careful, Marty. I'll call you back in a couple of days, okay? I'm only going to be here another week or so and I hope I can help out Amy Sanders by then."

I hung up the phone and leaned against the wall, watching people come and go from Jack's parking lot. How well I remembered what it was like, locked in an animal cage and waiting to die. I could still hear the noises Lynda made as she prepared the crematory chamber to take me and Brad, her husband. Henry had slipped into the room and closed her in the chamber, then somehow managed to turn on the crematory. It was warm here in the sun, but I shivered. I couldn't imagine a more ghastly death. She had been responsible for the deaths of scores of dogs and of at least one human being, though, so I did not mourn her.

A sea gull squawked, startling me out of my reverie. I looked at my watch again. I just had time to get back to Lola's for a bite of lunch and spend some time on the Internet before I went to meet with Eve.

CHAPTER 20

▼

"Amy and I went to the store. Sandwiches in the 'fridge," said Lola's note on the kitchen table. Munching a tuna fish sandwich, I plugged in my laptop computer. Lola had just joined the computer age and I had even gotten a couple of emails from her. But, I did not want to leave any tracks behind in her system; I didn't want anybody knowing what info I was going to look for online.

I waited through the usual few honks, beeps, and screeches that told me I was online. I went to AOL.com and punched in my password. I had never tried this before, but I was gratified to see the 'Welcome, M. Jackson' greeting. I was in my AOL account. I went to my mailbox and threw away a pile of spam that was knee deep. Then I went to YAHOO and tapped on the link for a reverse phone book. I punched in the number I had gotten from Audrey's phone, hit send, and crossed my fingers.

And there is was: 555 6752 was the number of a public phone at a gas station in Ilwaco, a small town to the south of Ocean Side at the base of the North Beach Peninsula by the mouth of the Columbia River. That was little or no help. But, I suppose a trip to Ilwaco would be in the offing anyway. A clue was a clue, after all.

Henry was sound asleep on my bed. I was glad. He would probably not be welcome in the library and I didn't want to make myself too well-remembered there anyway. It was 1:30. I better get going.

All I needed was a quick glance at the phone book and I had the address for the library. I was glad to see a street map in the front of the book too, now I knew where to go.

It was a cute little library, located in a large, old house. Once inside, I could see why Eve suggested it as a meeting place. The building was three stories tall with a basement and full of books in what had been bedrooms, living room, dining room, and all the other rooms in a house. There were lots of little nooks and crannies where she and I would be able to talk without being observed.

The front counter was deserted, a sign reading "Tap bell for assistance" sat next to a silver bell. There was a computer on the counter and the message on the screen. It said, "Can't find your book? Enter title or type." I moved the mouse and the message disappeared, replaced with a page entitled Find The Book. I entered the word cookbook in the blank space and hit the enter key.

Third floor, northeast corner room, was my answer. I headed for the stairs.

The northeast corner room probably had been a bedroom. One wall had shelves of cookbooks, there were sewing, decorating, and home improvement books on the rest of the walls. Beside the cookbook shelf was a dormer window, where a cushion had been added to tempt a reader. Unable to stop myself, I pulled a quilting book from the shelf and sat down to read.

"Maggie?" came a whisper. I jerked my head up, whacking myself on the slanted ceiling of the dormer.

"I'm sorry. I didn't mean to scare you." Eve stood in front of me, wringing her hands.

"That's okay, Eve. Serves me right for getting so wound up in this." I said, putting the quilting book back on the shelf.

Eve picked up a cookbook that featured bread. She checked the index then opened the book. "I have to copy a recipe before we talk. Dick will be expecting me to bring one home." She went to the Xerox machine in the corner of the room and dropped a dime in to make her copy. The paper dropped into the copier tray. Eve folded it carefully and put it in her pocket. Then she looked around; she didn't want us to be seen together, that was obvious.

"Good job on the phone this morning," I said. "But why didn't you want Dick to know you were going to be seeing me?"

"He's very jealous and if he thinks I'm doing anything wrong…" she let her voice dwindle and shrugged. "He can be hard to live with."

"Eve, does he ever hit you?"

"No, but he has threatened to. I confess—I am afraid of him."

"That's no way to live. Are you happy with him otherwise?"

Great. Now I had Eve in tears. "No, not really, but I don't know how I would survive alone."

"The same way you did before you married him," I said. "Don't let him bully you, Eve. Now, I'm hoping you have more to tell me about the Armstrongs."

"Yes." Eve dried her eyes and sat up straighter, looking determined. "Just before Dick came in yesterday I was going to tell you about Carl Rolley."

If I'd had antennae they would be waving around now. Again Carl Rolley's name comes up.

"I met him earlier today, at Audrey Holt's place. He seems nice enough," I said.

"I'm not sure about him," Eve said. "Sometimes he sort of scares me. But then, it seems like a lot of things do these days. Sometimes I feel like I'm living in some strange country where I don't speak the language. It doesn't make sense; I grew up around here." She shook her head.

"Anyway, about Carl. He was always hanging around at the Armstrong's. George was kind of crippled up and Carl seemed to be there a lot helping him. Sometimes, though, it seemed like George didn't want him there; I could hear them arguing."

"Did anything happen that you remember the day before the Armstrongs disappeared?"

"I know Carl was there 'most all day. George had been gone and Bethel was there by herself. I heard her telling Carl to leave George's stuff alone, to not try and work with the drill press until George got back. Carl called her a stupid old hag and said something like it wouldn't matter for much longer anyway. But, then he left."

I felt a prickle of fear go down my back. It sounded like Carl knew a lot about the Armstrongs. I was going to have to talk to him again.

"Did anything else happen?"

Eve nodded. "I saw George come home. He went into the little shop that he had built on the side of the trailer, then he came out as fast as he could and went into the trailer. I couldn't hear what he said, but when they came out I heard Bethel say, 'What do you mean, it's gone?' and George said, 'It's just not there. Was Carl here today?' When Bethel said yes, George said he was going to call the cops. But, I guess he didn't, because nobody came by."

"Do you have any idea what was missing from George's shop?"

"No, and I never got a chance to find out because the next day they were gone." Eve stood up. "I need to go. Dick will be expecting me back."

"Wait just a minute," I said. "What happened after the Armstrongs were gone. What happened to all their things?"

"I don't know. I saw Carl around there a few times, but with them gone there was nobody to pay him, so he quit coming by. After a while a moving company came and hauled the trailer away. Carl started driving George's car, he told me George had sold it to him just before they left town."

If that were true, why was Carl driving an old Ford Galaxy? I wondered. Eve was getting more nervous the longer we talked. I did not want her at risk of being hurt by her husband if she were gone too long.

"Thanks for coming and talking to me, Eve. If you think of anything else, call me at Lola's." I wrote the number on the back of another of my cards and gave it to her.

"I hope you find Bethel and George," she said. "I talked a little bit to Amy and she is very nice. I have to go. Good-bye." Eve hurried down the stairs and out of the little library. I sat and thought for a few minutes. I never had talked to the two sisters that lived across the street from George and Bethel. I would swing by their place again right now.

CHAPTER 21

▼

This time when I got to the Olsen's house there was a car in the driveway. I went up the walk, marveling at the flowers in the gardens that edged the walk and stretched across the front of the house on both sides of the porch. I tapped on the door.

The elderly lady that answered the door looked like a puff of wind would blow her away. Her face was nearly skeletal and her arm looked like a twig. But, bright blue eyes flashed out of deep sockets and her voice was firm.

"Yes?" she said.

I was sick to death of telling the tale, but once again I introduced myself and told Amy's story. After I was done she stood still for a moment, then pushed the screen door open.

"You had better come in; this is not something we want to talk about on the porch."

"Sylvia!" she yelled into the house. "We got company. I'm Hester, by the way."

Within moments we were joined by a lady who looked enough like Hester to be her twin. "No, we aren't twins, we just look alike," were Sylvia's first words to me.

"And you must be a mind reader, too," I said. "I was thinking you must be twins."

"Come on in and sit down," said Hester. "I just put the tea on; would you like a cup?"

Tea sounded wonderful and within moments I was sipping a well-brewed cup and nibbling on tiny cookies. I looked around the living room. Polished, dark mahogany side tables held lovely china figurines. The furniture was richly upholstered in fabric that felt like velvet, the assorted jewel tone colors gleaming through the lace antimacassars covering the headrest area and the arms of the chairs. My chair was a deep purple, Hester sat in crimson, and Sylvia chose forest green. Both ladies were dressed in crisp housedresses, they looked like identical Donna Reed grandmothers. I felt like I was having tea with royalty. When the tea was gone, Sylvia gave Hester a steady look. "Well, are you going to tell her about it or shall I?"

Hester frowned. "I'm getting to it. So," she said, turning to face me, "You are looking for George and Bethel Armstrong, too."

"Yes I am. Is there someone else trying to find them?"

"Yes, but he wasn't really looking for Bethel and George. A young man, he said he was an insurance agent, was looking for Bethel and George's daughter, but she hadn't gotten to town yet. We didn't know anything about her and so we had nothing we could tell him."

"We heard that she is in town now, but, well, we haven't called the man. Here's his card," Sylvia said, holding out a business card.

"Why haven't you called him or told Amy that he was here?"

"That fat sheriff told us we'd better keep our noses out of what he called 'his business' or we'd be sorry. That made us really mad, but we feel trapped," Hester said.

Sylvia spoke up again. "Just look at us. It wouldn't take much if we broke a hip or an arm and that would mean the end of us. Besides, Oliver told us that Bethel was having trouble with George, that he was losing his memory and maybe he had Alzheimer's. Oliver said that George kept calling in reports of things being stolen, but when he would investigate, nothing was missing."

"So we weren't sure if Oliver was right or not," said Hester, "But now that their daughter is here and hasn't heard from them, and, well, we are getting worried."

"Are you going to figure out if anything happened to them? Is that why you're here?" asked Sylvia.

"That's what I'm trying to do," I said. "Thank you, ladies, for talking to me. If you think of anything else, you know where I'm staying. I hope to find something soon; I only plan on being here another week or so."

I went back to Lola's and put Henry on his leash. He needed to dig in the sand and I needed to think.

CHAPTER 22

▼

There were a few puffy clouds being pushed along by the wind, but it was otherwise a clear, beautiful day. After Henry had finished his duty and I had cleaned up after him, I started walking toward the end of the peninsula. It was too far away to get all the way to the end before the tide came in and there was a bird sanctuary there, too. Henry would not be appreciated. But, we walked for on a ways. It was quiet, only a wheeling sea gull's cries were louder than the sounds of the ocean. On the weekends the beach would be teeming with people, kids, and dogs, but now I had the sand to myself.

We walked for about half an hour, Henry fascinated by everything, me thinking about what I had learned, and how little that actually was. A flock of sandpipers came out of the tules and I stopped to watch them run about, picking up some sort of snack out of the wet sand. I turned around and we started back down the beach. The tide was coming in and I wanted to get back before it was all the way in. It was much easier to walk on the firm wet sand than the squishy dry stuff.

On the way back the wind was blowing in my face, so instead of watching the ocean, I looked at the houses that had been built just above the tules. I wondered what it was like for them during big storms. I had seen some amazing weather in past trips. One house looked very new; the cedar shakes were still a brownish color. After years of exposure to the salt air they would become that lovely silvery-gray color seen on the older homes. It was a pretty place that looked like it belonged there on the beach, rather than some of the fancy villas I had passed. I turned back for another glance after Henry and I had passed it and a flash of electric blue from an open garage door caught my attention.

I stopped and stared. I could see the front end of a truck and it looked just like the one that Amy had described to me that her dad used to pull the trailer. I walked closer, trying to see if this indeed was a Chevrolet.

A side door opened on the house and a man stepped out. His hair was gray, but he walked with a spring in his step. Seeing me standing there staring at his garage, he waved and called out. "Hello! How are you today?"

I continued up the sand toward him. "I'm fine. I sure like your house."

A woman had joined him and she called out, "Thanks! We like it too."

"Dan Carson," he said, holding out his hand, "And this is my wife, Susan."

"I'm glad to meet you. I'm Maggie Jackson and this is Henry." Henry walked over and sat down in front of the Carsons, waiting for the petting he assumed would be coming. "He has become quite the beach cat in the short time we've been here."

"We have a dog that loves to chase the waves. He's sleeping right now and he'll be unhappy to have missed you. He actually likes cats."

"That's really a bright shade of blue on your truck," I said, pointing.

"Yes, isn't that something?" said Susan. "On one of our first days here we were driving around looking at all the different houses and we saw this guy standing out in his yard with this truck in the driveway. There was a for sale sign on the windshield and Dan just stopped on a whim and asked the guy how much he wanted for it."

"I still feel like we stole it," said Dan. "This truck in only a few years old and he sold it to us for $2000."

"Why so cheap?" I asked.

"Well," said Susan, "He said he was just in town clearing out his parents' place. They had died in a boating accident and he was just trying to get everything taken care of quickly, as he needed to go home and get back to work."

"I was a little worried at first if this was on the up and up," said Dan, "Because the guy wanted cash rather than a check. But, I didn't have any trouble when I went to transfer the title, so it must have been okay."

"Do you happen to remember who you bought it from?"

Dan shook his head. "No, I don't. He was a tall, skinny guy, with longish red hair. I don't think I even paid that much attention to the name on the title. Susan, do you know?"

She shook her head.

"Do you remember where the house was where you got the truck?"

"No, we were just driving around. All I remember is the lovely gardens around the house across the street," said Susan. "Why so curious about our truck, anyway?"

That sounded like the Olsen sisters' house and that red hair, had to be Carl Rolley, again popping up in the midst of all this.

"A friend of mine asked me to help her find her parents. She had been invited to come stay with them for awhile, but when she got here they were gone. She told me her dad bought a truck like this to haul their motor home."

"Maybe that's the couple that drowned," Dan said. I wonder if she was the sister of the man we dealt with?"

"But wouldn't she have been notified by her brother if that were so and that had been her folks that died?" asked Susan.

"You would think so," he said. "Oh, well, it must have been somebody different. It's been nice talking to you—stop by again some time and meet the dog." Dan and Susan went back into their house and Henry and I started back toward Lola's, my thoughts swirling around this new information.

CHAPTER 23

▼

There is something enervating about sea air. I had hardly finished dinner when I got so sleepy it seemed the only cure was to go to bed. I crawled under the covers with the thought of visiting the town of Ilwaco the next day to see what I could find out at the public phone booth.

I felt like I had just fallen asleep, but the clock said 2:30. I was wide awake, being taunted by a fragment of a dream. Suddenly I remembered what I had been dreaming about. It was the insurance man, looking for Amy. Why would an insurance agent be looking for her unless it was to settle a claim, like a life insurance benefit? Sylvia and Hester had shown me a card. Had I given it back to them? I could not remember. I got up and clicked on the bedside lamp. The shorts I had worn were on the chair. I reached out and grabbed them.

Stephen Wilmore, agent, Amica Insurance. There was a phone number and hooray! an email address. I couldn't wait. I grabbed my laptop and powered it up.

After writing a note to Stephen Wilmore I was able to go back to sleep. Morning would hopefully bring some answers. I snuggled back under the covers, Henry muttering a mild protest at being disturbed, and I drifted off to sleep.

When I woke up again the sun was shining. Except for the usual fantastic offers and other assorted spam, my email box was empty. Oh, well, it had only been about six hours since I wrote to Stephen Wilmore. I deleted all the junk mail and signed off. I would go to Ilwaco and see what I could learn, then check online again when I got back.

Ilwaco is a small town that sits at the base of the North Beach Peninsula. It is one of the many towns around the peninsula that makes a great deal of its living from sport and commercial fishermen. There were several charter companies, some as small as a guy with a boat, others running a fleet of boats. Some people liked to go out beyond the bar at the mouth of the Columbia River into the ocean proper for salmon, halibut, and other seafood, depending on the season. Others liked to fish for sturgeon in the river, and some people just walked out onto the jetty, poles in hand. There is a commercial cannery on the docks where fresh fish was for sale, too. The entire area was fragrant with fish and salt water. It was a clear, sunny day and the water sparkled.

The convenience store listed as the location of the phone number I had gotten from Audrey's phone was near the docks. It was hard for me to think about Amy and her problems with so much activity going on. I could stand all day and watch the boats come and go. Every kind and size of boat, from rowboats with small outboard motors to fancy, tarted-up inboards that were more like floating houses, were coming and going in the marina. There were boats belonging to men who fished for a living, too, and those were my favorites. There was nothing on them for decorative purposes, everything had a function, but they had a unique beauty anyway. I stood on the dock and watched for a few minutes, then tore myself away to go see what I could learn.

Which didn't turn out to be much. There was so much activity and with so many people coming and going all the time, the odds of anybody noticing somebody making a phone call weren't even slim, they were none. I talked to several people, but nobody had seen anything. This was a pointless waste of time as far as finding Amy's parents went, but I enjoyed my time in Ilwaco anyway. I decided to go back to Ocean Side and check my email again.

On the way back up the peninsula I had to go through the town of Long Beach. I had missed it on the way down, but now I spotted the fabric store. No way could I not stop.

Several dollars later, I forced myself to get back in the Blazer. I had a nice new stack of fabrics though. Maybe I would start a project while I was here. I had brought one rotary cutter and a cutting mat along with my Singer Featherweight sewing machine. I never knew when a quilt attack might happen and I liked to be prepared.

Back at Lola's, I tossed my new fabric into the washer on a short cycle. It would be ready for me soon if I needed it. I went to my room and got my computer up and running and signed on to AOL. There was a note from Stephen Wilmore in my email box. He wrote that he was thrilled that I knew Amy Sanders and asked me to have her call him as soon as possible. He said that he was looking for her to talk to her about a life insurance policy. Her parents had gone out on a charter fishing trip, he wrote. A storm had come up and the boat had nearly sunk. Both Bethel and George had been swept overboard and were presumed drowned.

Now I was going to have to tell Amy that it looked like her parents were dead, that they had drowned. No insurance company would be wanting to pay out benefits unless they were sure of the facts. I could hear Amy in the kitchen with Lola. She sounded cheerful and happy. I sat on the bed, watching my computer screen fade to black. It took a mental talking-to before I could make my self stand up and head to the kitchen. I was going to have to destroy Amy's bit of happiness and I hated the thought.

I walked into the kitchen and handed Amy Stephen Wilmore's card. "I emailed him after the Olsen sisters gave me his card," I said. "They told me he was here looking for you."

"Why would an insurance guy want me?" Amy said.

I looked at Lola. From her face I could tell she knew where the conversation was going. She sank into a chair and waited.

"He was looking for you because his company had been notified of the deaths of your mom and dad. He has life insurance benefits for you."

Amy's face went white. Lola jumped up and put her arm around Amy's shoulders. "Here, sit down. Maggie, grab her some water."

"I'm all right. I want to know, what happened?" Amy said, her voice shaking.

"I don't have all the details; I will get those for you, but it seems that they went out into the ocean on a fishing charter. There was a storm and they were lost overboard. I guess the boat nearly sank before it made it back over the bar," I said.

Amy sat still, her hands clenched into fists. "I don't believe it," she said.

"I know it's hard…"

"No," she interrupted me, "I mean I don't believe it at all. My dad was not a fisherman, he didn't like it, and my mom would almost get seasick in a swimming pool. There would have been no way she would have gone out in a boat, for any reason."

"Are you sure?" said Lola. "Lots of people who have never wanted to go fishing before suddenly decide that want to, when they see all that water and all the neat equipment."

"That might be true for my dad," Amy said, "But I *know* my mother wouldn't have gone with him. She wouldn't even get in a rowboat. This is a lie."

"Well, let's talk with this Stephen Wilmore as soon as we can," I said. "He should have all the details and we can find out just what is going on. It's too late today, his office is on the east coast and is closed by now, but I'll go email him and ask him to call us first thing in the morning. That's about all we can do for now."

I went to Lola's laundry room and tossed my new fabric into the dryer with a Bounce sheet. New fabric was crisp and nice with all that sizing in it, but I always feared the colors running or the fabric stretching or shrinking in a funny way. If any of that was going to happen I wanted it to be before I used it in a quilt. Henry was hungry, so I fed him and then helped Lola fix dinner. Amy just sat and watched us, looking shell-shocked.

After we ate I was restless. I had all this new fabric, some heavenly blues, greens, and yellows. I would play around with some nine-patch blocks, I decided. Teaching that class had reminded me of all the different patterns you could achieve with this simple little quilt block. I had just gotten Marti Michell's book 101 Nine Patch Quilts and had been stunned at the variety of arrangements using those simple blocks.

I had ironed the fabric and cut out several strips of each color, each one 2 ½ inches wide and across the width of the fabric from selvedge to selvedge, which was about 42 inches, when Amy wandered in.

"What are you making?"

I was glad to have her show an interest in something, maybe this would take her mind off her troubles. I felt my teaching mode kick in.

"These are strips of fabric that I'm going to cut up into squares. I'll put those squares together to make a quilt block called a nine patch."

"Why is it called a nine patch?"

"Because each block is made up of nine individual patches of fabric, usually in two different colors, or one dark and one light of the same color. You sew them so the block looks like a checkerboard, first row dark-light-dark, second row light-dark-light, and the third row dark-light-dark."

"But how do you do that with those strips?"

"After I have enough of the nine patch blocks, I can figure out all different sorts of ways to put them together to make a finished quilt. Each little square is 2 ½ by 2 ½ inches, because ¼ inch is the seam allowance you use. After you sew the small squares together the finished block will be 6½ x 6½ inches. And after you sew it to the other blocks the ¼ inch is taken off all the sides for the seams, so the block is 6x6 inches in the finished quilt and each small square is 2x2 inches.* Are you with me so far?"

She nodded, so I went on. "As you make each row of the nine patch, sewing three squares together alternating the colors, you need to press it. The seams are ironed to one side, usually toward the darker fabric, rather than open seams like in sewing clothing. This is to help prevent the batting from "bearding," or sticking up through, the seam lines in the finished quilt. After I have made three strips of three squares each, two that are dark-light-dark and one that is light-dark-light, and pressed them, I sew them together. See how the seams end up that are pressed in opposite directions? It keeps the seams from being too bulky in the finished quilt and they are easier to keep lined up when you put the little strips together, too. I use a pin to hold the seams together, though." I held up my first nine patch for Amy to look at.

"I get it," she said, "That looks pretty easy and I love those colors, too."

"It is easy. Now carefully iron it flat from the right side and your first nine patch block is done."

"That is really simple, isn't it? It looks like fun, too. I've never made a quilt, but now I think maybe I want to try one," said Amy.

I cut more strips of fabric and Amy got busy. It only took her a few minutes to become comfortable with the ¼ inch seam, which looks so narrow compared to the ⅝ inch seam used for sewing clothing. Soon she had a stack of 10 completed blocks. I left her arranging them in different ways, trying to decide on a final design for her quilt. She decided to make a lap size quilt, one that would be about 48 inches by 60 inches, 4 by 5 feet. This is a good size, she could actually use it as an extra blanket on her bed if she wanted to, but it wasn't so large that she would get discouraged by all the blocks she would need. With a six-inch outer border and a three-inch frame around her block arrangement, she would need to make 35 nine patch blocks. If she chose a design where a solid block alternated with the nine patch, which can be lovely, she would only need to make 18 nine patch blocks and cut out 17 blocks of one of the plain fabrics. I heard Amy humming under her breath as I left the room. Nothing like a little fabric play to cheer a person up.

* See the end of the book for basic instructions for this quilt.

CHAPTER 24

▼

The next morning I found Amy still arranging and rearranging her blocks. She had made a few more nine patch blocks and I could see from the way she had laid them out that she was thinking about using some solid color blocks, too. "You weren't up all night, were you?" I asked her.

She laughed. "No, but I had to force myself to go to bed—I was having so much fun. What do I do after I decide what my pattern will be?"

"Putting it all together, which is really the easy part. Deciding on fabrics and a design is the tough stuff. Once you have all your blocks done you will sew them together in rows, then you will sew those rows together to make the center of your quilt. Next, you will cut pieces as long as the sides of the quilt of whatever fabric you want for an outside border. Sometimes I put a narrower piece of fabric all around the center first, for sort of a frame effect, then put the outer border on. You sew the side pieces on, then measure and cut pieces for the top and bottom. You will also need fabric for binding, which is the last step. I like to use the same fabric as the frame piece, if I do one, but that is up to you. You could use one of the fabrics from the nine patches or use the same fabric as your solid color blocks. After you are done with the top we will need to get you some fabric for the back. I can take it home with me and quilt it for you and mail it to you when it is done."

"Well, I have to pay you for all this material and your work, that's for sure," said Amy. "How much will it be?"

"Tell you what. We can go back to the fabric store in Long Beach. You can replace the fabric that you used of mine, and you can choose fabric for your back piece, the border, and the binding. I have batting at home, you can just pay me for the yard or so of that I will use and I'll send you a bill for the quilting and postage. How does that sound? That way, you pay just a little at a time." And I won't be charging you much for the quilting, I thought.

"But I can't even buy fabric now," she said, tears forming in her eyes. "I don't have any money with me, just my debit card and I have to be careful I don't run out of money until I can find another job or go back home."

"Don't worry about it. You can send it to me later; we'll just go and replace the fabric, then you will know how much you owe me. I bet you'll be good for it. Let's go grab some breakfast. Then I think we need to call on Sheriff Krupe and see why he didn't tell you about your parents drowning."

"Okay," she said, "We can go see him. But, first I want to talk to the guy whose boat my mom and dad were supposedly on. I still can't believe my mother would get on a boat. Do you know his name?"

"No, I don't. Let's try calling this Stephen Wilmore and see if he can tell us anything more."

Stephen Wilmore was in his office. "I was just about to call you," he said.

"Hold on," I said, "I'll let you talk to Amy Sanders."

Amy sat and listened for a few minutes. I heard her say, "Okay, thank you. That will be fine. I'll let you know if I need anything more from you. Good-bye."

"He said he would fax copies here of the death certificates along with all the other information he has," said Amy, hanging up the phone. "Then he said I can call him when it is convenient for me if I have questions. Otherwise, he will send the paperwork to Chicago so I'll have it there when I go back."

We hoped he would send the faxes quickly. Lola went in and sat by the machine, Amy at her side. They stared at it, willing in it to ring. I was glad when it rang almost immediately.

"These sure look authentic," I told Amy, as the paper oozed out of the fax machine. The certificates were not in color, of course, but I could see the notary's seal and recognized the paper, it reminded me of the type of paper that money was printed on, with little lines in the background and an ornate design to prevent counterfeiting.

"I don't care," she said, sounding determined. "Until I talk to the man that they were supposedly with and he can give me some real proof, I won't believe any piece of paper—no matter how good it looks. Besides, look at this," she pointed to the date of death. "This says my mom and dad died on the same day I was coming to visit? Why would they go fishing, if they were expecting me to arrive on that day? Let's go talk to that fisherman guy, what's his name?"

"Well, there's a Gary Wilson listed as the owner of The Sea Ghost, the fishing boat they chartered on the day they drowned, if they really did," I said. Amy's determination was rubbing off on me. "I suppose the next thing we could do would be to go to Ilwaco and track him down."

"Let's go now," Amy said, jumping up and heading for the door.

It was another beautiful day on the Washington peninsula, where so much of the year it was rainy. I could see some clouds in the west though, and I wondered if a storm were in the offing.

By the time we got to Ilwaco many of the professional fishermen had left for the day. Most of the tourist charter boats were still at the docks, though. They weren't as busy in the middle of the week as on the weekends.

"Where do we start?" Amy asked.

"I don't know," I said, "I suppose we can just go to the moorages and ask."

It took us most of the morning, but we were able to talk to people at every commercial dock in Ilwaco. At noon we staggered into a small café and ordered lunch, both starved and exhausted after our search. What made us even more tired and discouraged was that nobody we talked to in Ilwaco had heard of either Gary Wilson or The Sea Ghost.

"Maybe it really is a ghost ship," said Amy. "I don't understand any of this."

Neither did I. Where did Stephen Wilmore get his information? Was Amy right? Had her parents not gone out on a fishing trip and drowned? I was beginning to think this way, too. We sat for a few minutes spooning up hot, creamy clam chowder.

"So, what do we do now?" Amy asked.

"Well, I guess we need to go back to Ocean Side and talk to the sheriff again. I can't believe he didn't know about this, and if he did, why didn't he just tell you? At least that explains why this Stephen Wilmore couldn't contact you; you had already left on your trip by the time he tried to call. Have you checked your voice mail since you left home?"

"No. I didn't figure it would matter. There shouldn't have been any important calls coming in." Amy laughed, then her laugh turned into a sob. "Who knew?"

Our bowls were empty and only crumbs remained from our sandwiches. "We might as well head back," I said. "Do you still want to stop at the fabric store in Long Beach?"

"You bet I do," she said, drying her eyes. "At least I can feel like I accomplished *something* today."

CHAPTER 25

▼

After a happy interlude in the fabric store in Long Beach we were back in Ocean Side. Amy carefully tucked away the receipt from the fabric she had replaced for me and for the fabric for the back, frame, and border of her quilt. I knew I would get paid back as soon as the mystery of her parents was solved and she got back home. It had been a tough day, though. Amy was excited to get back to Lola's and finish the rest of the nine patch blocks she needed for her quilt, but then she would sigh and stare silently out the car window, saddened by the morning's events.

We pulled up in front of the Ocean Side Town Hall/Sheriff's Office and Amy got out and went in while I locked the Blazer. As I walked in the door I heard Sheriff Krupe's voice say, in a really bad W.C. Fields imitation, "What can I do for you, my little chickadee?"

Amy had been looking at the wanted posters on the wall and he had not recognized her from the back. She turned around and he frowned.

"Oh, it's you again. What do you want now?"

"Why didn't you tell me that my parents drowned? How come you kept insisting that they had just moved away?"

Oliver Krupe glared at her then turned to me. "What are you doing here? You encouraging her to mess around all this time?"

This guy was beyond belief. Either he was totally stupid or crooked beyond words. Why would he hide this information from Amy? What would be the point? He looked away from her, sweat popping out on his forehead. He coughed and covered his mouth, then started to rub his nose. He was going to lie to us, I just knew it, and he wouldn't be very good at it, either.

"That's because I just found out about it today. I hadn't had a chance to catch up on all the accident reports and they are slow about reporting stuff to me from Ilwaco. I was going to call you later on and let you know. But, I really did think they had just moved away."

"An insurance agent was here looking for Amy several days ago, Sheriff. He did come and talk to you, didn't he?" I said.

"I don't remember talking to any insurance guy. And if he told you he did come see me, he's lying. Those people drowned, period."

Amy stared at him. "We went to Ilwaco today, Sheriff. We could not find any trace of the fisherman or the boat that they supposedly went out on. I really think something has happened to them. My mom would never go out on a boat, she gets too seasick and my dad doesn't like to fish. I know something else happened and it's your job to help me find out what that was and where they are. I don't believe what these say at all," she said, flourishing the death certificates at him.

Good girl, Amy. Sweat was running down Oliver Krupe's face now and he had gotten increasingly red as she talked. "Well, I ain't doin' squat. We have here in the office certified copies of genuine death certificates. As far as I'm concerned this case is closed—not that there ever was a case in the first place. Now get out of here, both of you. I got work to do." He patted his pistol, unsnapping and snapping the strap that held it in place in his holster.

Amy stared at him for a minute. She said, "I'll be back when I figure out what happened and then you will be sorry you didn't help me." She turned on her heel and marched out of the office. I followed her.

We went back to Lola's and headed for the patio. But, a storm was coming and the patio would be a soggy place to sit. Black clouds were heading toward the beach, their edges a strange greenish-yellow color. The wind had picked up and spray was blowing off the tops of the waves as the tide headed in. The kitchen was a lot cozier.

"Is it possible that these are fakes?" said Amy, tapping her fingers on the copies of the death certificates we had gotten from Steve Wilmore.

"I suppose so, but who would do that, and why?" I said. "Were your parents rich?"

"No, not really. They sold their Chicago apartment for quite a bit, but spent most of that money on the truck, the trailer, and the piece of property here. My dad liked to carry some cash, but it would not have been a huge amount."

But maybe enough to be tempting. I kept thinking about Carl Rolley. It sounded like he had sold the Armstrong's truck, how he was able to do that without the title being transferred to him I did not know. But, I suppose it wouldn't be hard to forge a signature, assuming you got hold of that title. And how did the trailer get sold, or the property either, for that matter? So many legalities to get around. But, if you knew a crooked cop who would like some extra money…Oliver Krupe's face loomed in my mind. Maybe it was time to take a closer look at him.

CHAPTER 26

▼

The threatened storm had turned out to be not much of one after all. We had a flood of rain for a while, and a blustery wind, then the skies cleared. By the next morning the air was washed clean and the sea sparkled. Amy was snipping and sewing, so I decided to go sniff around the sheriff a little.

It was easy to find Oliver Krupe's house; his address was listed in the slim Ocean Side telephone book. I drove there to take a look. The house didn't look particularly fancy, like many here near the ocean the cedar siding had silvered after the exposure to the salt air, but it still would have been costly. This was prime real estate here on the Willapa Bay side of the peninsula with the property right on the water. I drove by the house then parked the Blazer and got out to walk around, Henry on his leash at my side.

We exchanged pleasantries with people cleaning up the debris the previous night's wind had blown into their yards and nobody seemed too curious about us strolling slowly along the edge of the road. When we got to the house next door to Krupe's the owner was out sweeping her sidewalk.

"Would you mind if we walked down to the water here?" I asked her. "My cat just loves all the fishy smells."

"Please, feel free," she said. "That is certainly an unusual cat, walking on a leash like that."

"Yes, he is one in a million, that's for sure. Thanks for letting us invade your property. We won't hang around too long."

The woman laughed. "I would hardly call one black cat an invasion. Take all the time you want; it's such a lovely day."

Henry was pulling hard on his leash. I had told her the truth, he did love to nose around on the sand. This water wouldn't be coming to get him; he might like it even better here than on the ocean beach side of the peninsula.

When we got onto the sand I walked Henry back and forth a little bit. I didn't want to get too close to the Krupe place, but I was curious about a boat I could see tied to the dock floating in the quiet water behind the property. I stood and gazed out onto the bay for a few minutes. The tide was out and Henry was fascinated by all the debris that had been left behind by the water. He sniffed and dug and had a great time. I found a dry piece of driftwood and sat down on it to watch him. Soon he felt he had answered all his questions and he started back my direction. Then a sea gull landed on the sand near the Krupe's dock.

Henry instantly became a predator. He dropped to his stomach and flattened his ears, then started a sneak attack. He oozed along the sand, then froze, hoping the gull had not seen him. Then he dashed ahead a few feet and dropped back to his stomach. I knew his eyes were wide open, the pupils dilated. His jaw was probably vibrating, too, like it did when he got excited or mad. The gull ignored him, and Henry continued to sneak toward it.

I released the catch on the leash. He would be able to go about 20 feet before getting to the end of the line. I knew he would never be able to catch the gull, but I had watched him chase enough birds at home that I knew what he would do after trying. His habit could help me snoop while looking innocent to anybody who might be watching me.

He crept across the sand, whiskers forward and eyes wide open. Suddenly he charged, leaping up into the air and flaying around with his paws, white claws out and ready. The gull hopped up into the air, screaming raucous insults. Henry had missed him by a mile. Henry plopped back into the sand. He didn't even glance in my direction, but just started a bath. After all, this posture said, this is what I intended to do in the first place, jump into the air then have a grooming session.

"Come on, Henry, let's go." I called to him. As I knew he would, he ignored me. I called him a couple of more times and tugged on his leash, then frowned and shook my head, trying to look disgusted. Wondering if I were being observed, I walked over to him. "You just never learn, do you? No way could you catch a sea gull." I leaned down to pick him up and took the opportunity to take the best look I could at the Krupe's dock.

The boat I had seen looked like a pretty fancy speed boat and I knew they didn't come cheap. Henry looked at the boat, too, and the fur along his backbone stood up in a stickley spike. He didn't like the look of the Krupe's place, either.

On our way back to the street I was able to get a look at the front of the Krupe's garage. Their driveway wound around the house and the garage doors faced the bay. The doors were reinforced with heavy hinges and there was a very impressive padlock securing them. There was a window in the side of the garage facing the neighbor's house, but I could see that it had been covered from the inside. "I wonder what's hidden in there, Henry. Sure wish I could peek in."

I waved my thanks to the lady in her yard and Henry and I strolled back up to the Blazer. "So, kitty, Oliver Krupe has an expensive boat. Their house is nothing fancy, but even a tar-paper shack goes for a big price here on the water. Do you suppose he has some other source for an income? And how in the world could I find that out?"

I tucked Henry in his carrier and he looked at me and bobbed his head. "Meow," he said.

CHAPTER 27

▼

I felt at loose ends. I didn't know what to do next, where to turn. So, I turned toward Oysterville. I bought a quart of fresh-shucked oysters. I hoped Amy liked them, as I was going to bread and fry them for dinner. I knew that Lola liked them, but that was a requirement of living here on the coast.

"If you're going to cut them open, don't look at them," said Lola with a laugh at Amy's expression.

Amy closed her eyes and put the piece of oyster in her mouth. It was my turn to laugh now, watching her grimace of distaste turn into wonderment. "These are *good!*" she said.

"What, did you think we would try to poison you?" I looked at the empty platter. Next time I had better get two quarts.

We took our coffee out to the living room. "I learned a couple of things today," I said. "The sheriff has a pretty nice house on the bay side of the peninsula, right on the water, and what looks like a fancy speed boat tied up to his dock. There's a locked garage that I would love to take a peek into, also. Does he have a Rolls Royce parked in there?"

"No, it's not a Rolls," said Lola, "But you aren't the first person to be curious about that garage. Last year on Labor Day during the Rod Run to the End of the World he showed up in the parade of cars in a fully-restored 1936 Buick. He had fixed it up like an old police car, but like a hot rod police car, engine all chromed and fancy wheels and paint job. He told everybody that he got a good deal on it from an auction in Portland, Oregon. He said it was a car seized from a drug dealer."

"Do you believe him?" I asked.

"At the time I did, but after Mike Thompson, the previous sheriff, drowned in a boating accident, a lot of strange things have happened. I started to wonder if Oliver had something to do with that; the way he acted after it happened. Oliver was so bent on becoming sheriff, but he knew he would never win an election against Mike, who was one of those honest, caring, dependable people you so rarely meet these days. It seems like there have been so many drownings over the last few months, it just really makes me wonder. But, I have no proof of anything.

"Who would think that this sort of stuff could go on in sleepy little Ocean Side? But, I guess it's the same everywhere, always somebody ready to take advantage." Lola shook her head and sighed.

We all jumped at the sudden banging on the front door. Henry leaped to his feet and started across the floor, every black hair standing straight out. I picked him up and opened the door.

Oliver Krupe stood there in street clothes, but wearing his holster and gun. Before I could say a word he pushed himself into the house, nearly knocking me down.

"Rawr, grrrr," Henry roared at him and swung a black arm with claws unsheathed. Oliver jumped back and I was gratified to see his head hit the edge of the door. "Get that animal away from me," he yelled, "Or I'll run you in."

"You'll do nothing of the kind, Oliver Krupe. You pushed your way into my house and scared my niece's cat. How dare you threaten us. What in the hell do you want, anyway?"

Lola had come up behind me and all I could do was stare. Her hair had sprung out of its bun and was sticking straight out from her head. She looked as stickled as Henry did. This was only the second time I had heard her say anything much stronger than "Rats!" She must really be angry.

"You stay out of this, Lola. This is between me and her," he said, pointing at me.

"What do want with me?" you bag of shit, I wanted to add.

"What do you think you are doing, snooping around my house? My wife saw you, and I knew who it was when she told me about that fucking cat."

I was still holding Henry. His body was vibrating and I tell he was doing that funny thing with his teeth that he does when he's angry or hunting, like he was doing earlier while stalking the gull. It's sort of like very fast tooth chattering, without the sound. I could feel his jaws quivering. "Your house? I don't even know where you live."

"Oh, yes you do. My wife saw you—probably letting your damn cat crap on our beach."

"You mean over on the bay side?" I hoped he was buying my innocent act. "I had no idea that was your place." I turned to Lola and Amy. "I went for a walk this morning and I could tell Henry wanted to go exploring down by the water. A lady was out working in her yard, was that your house? Your flowers are beautiful," I was gushing now.

"No, that's the next door neighbors' place." He looked at me through slitted eyes. He seemed less sure. I hoped he bought my act. "What were you doing on my beach, then?"

"Henry took a dash at a sea gull. When he couldn't catch it he just sat down; that's what he always does when he tries to catch a bird and misses. I had to go pick him up."

Some of the red had faded from Oliver Krupe's face, but he still looked angry. "You just stay away from me and my place, you hear?"

"No problem, unless I need your professional help, of course?"

He puffed out his chest. "Of course, if you need the police, call. Good night, Lola."

She reached out and slammed the door shut behind him. "I don't know who he thinks he is, the king of this town? I'll sure be the first one to support anyone who runs against him in the next election." Her eyes flashed fire.

Amy had listened to us without interrupting, but now she said, "I'm getting scared, Maggie. Maybe we need to just let it go. I'll go home and try to put my life back together." She jumped to her feet. "But wait, if my parents were drowned, then their bodies must have been found by now. They must be at a funeral home or something. I'll need to arrange to have them sent home for burial. Tomorrow I need to find out." She walked out of the living room. "I'm going to go work on my quilt and then try and get some sleep. I'll see you both in the morning."

"Lola, I have never seen you so mad," I said after Amy left. "He really managed to push your buttons, didn't he."

"Oliver Krupe has been a bully ever since I first met him. I don't trust him one bit. If there's something fishy about Amy parents' deaths he would be the first one I would suspect."

"I'm wondering about him, too, and that Carl Rolley. From what I can figure out, Carl sold George Armstrong's truck to a couple that just built a house up the peninsula a ways, Susan and Dan Carson. I talked to them and the guy they described sure sounded like Carl."

"Carl and Oliver have always been, to use a cliché, as thick as thieves. Carl couldn't get a ticket in this town if he tried and Oliver has a handyman on call whenever he needs something done," said Lola.

"Carl probably is happy to do Oliver's dirty work, too," I said.

"That wouldn't surprise me a bit. But be careful around those two, Maggie, I wouldn't put much of anything past them."

Lola went off to bed and I went in and booted up my laptop. While I hated to bother him, if it hadn't have been for me and Rick, Marty Adams would never have been instrumental in breaking up the drug ring in the veterinary clinic. That had also netted him a fine cash reward, so what the heck, I would bother him.

I didn't have an email address for Marty, so I wrote to Rick, telling him everything I could think of about Amy, Oliver Krupe, the phantom fisherman Gary Wilson and his boat The Sea Ghost, and Carl Rolley. I asked Rick to ask Marty if he could get hold of original copies of the Armstrong's death certificates and determine if they were genuine. I also gave him Stephen Wilmore's name and phone number. I asked Rick to see if there was any way Marty could check on the sales of the truck and the land that the Armstrongs had. It was a long note, more of a tome, really, and it took me a couple of hours to get it all written down. By the time I was done I had no trouble falling asleep.

CHAPTER 28

▼

When I woke up to sunshine I lay for a minute and looked at the calendar hanging on the wall at the foot of the bed. It was almost the weekend. Then I would only have a week left of my scheduled stay. I hoped I could get Amy's questions answered by then.

I wouldn't count on Marty being able to do all I had asked, at least not immediately. He had his own job to worry about. Maybe I could learn something on my own. After all, land purchases were a part of public record. I would try the town hall—maybe there were some records there.

There was a young blond girl at the desk in the town hall. I had been glad to see that the sheriff's car was not parked in front of the police station that was on the other side of the town office. I would just as soon not have Oliver Krupe knowing what I was doing.

I didn't have the plat number or the actual address of the Armstrong's property, and even though the clerk blushed and ducked her head every time I spoke to her, when I told her the two intersecting streets it was easy for her to bring up the property number on her computer. She wrote it down for me then took me in the back.

"Here's all the records on all the property around here. It's not too well organized, but that property was sold within the last six months, so the papers should be in this file box." She handed me a box holding a stack of papers six inches thick. "There's a table over there," she said, pointing to the back of the room. "You can sit there and look for what you need."

"Clarice?" called a voice from the front, "Where are you?"

"That's my boss, I better go. Just put this back on the shelf when you are done, okay?" She turned and hurried off before I could answer her.

Clarice had certainly been right. This folder was just a hodge-podge of papers stuffed in every which way. It took me a awhile to figure out what each of the forms meant. I finally started stacks of the different kinds; it seemed there were four or five forms used each time a piece of property was bought or sold. Once that was done, I dug through one pile until I saw the name Armstrong. I did this with all the piles and soon I had found a complete record of their purchase of the property. That didn't interest me much, though. I really wanted to know who had bought the property from the Armstrongs, if they had actually sold it. I would have to start my search over, this time by the property number. This was harder, but after sneezing my way through the dusty piles of forms again, I found the first one with that specific number.

Oh, now here was something. "Guess who bought that piece of land," I muttered. "The infamous Carl Rolley. Now this is getting interesting."

It took me only a few minutes to find the rest of the forms for Carl Rolley's purchase of the Armstongs' property. I looked at the signatures. I wished I knew if those really were the hands of Bethel and George Armstrong. Amy might be able to tell, though, if I could get a copy to her.

Clarice's boss was continuing to talk to her in the front of the office. Then I heard their voices start to fade and muffled clumping sounds, like they were going up or down a flight of stairs. I looked out in the front and there was nobody there. A copy machine sat in one corner; did I dare try to copy these papers?

Clarice and her boss must be in the basement. I could hear noises under my feet and occasionally the sound of a voice. I scooped up the piles of papers I had made with either the Rolley or Armstrong name on them and praying that the floor would not squeak, I tiptoed over to the copy machine and dropped the papers into the feed tray. "C'mon, now, be a good quiet one," I whispered. I set it to make two copies of each page and pushed the start button.

It was a nice new machine, fast and silent. I was very happy about that, for as the last copy dropped I heard the voices from the basement getting louder. Clarice and her boss were on their way back up.

I scuttled back in the records room. I stuffed the copies I had made into the back waist band of my pants and jerked my shirt down over them. It was the best I could do; I had left my purse in the car. I had just finished putting the stacks of paper back in the file box when a short, fat, women came through the door.

"What are you doing back here?"

"I was just doing some research on a property sale."

"Why were you doing that?"

"A friend wanted to know who had sold her parents their land. They really liked this person and my friend wanted to use this same Realtor to help her buy a piece of property, too."

"That doesn't mean you can come snooping through my files."

"Oh, really? I thought all these sorts of transactions were part of the public record. Aren't they?"

She glared at me. She knew I was right, but she wasn't going to admit it. "How'd you get back here, anyway?"

"I brought her back, Melinda, I thought it was okay," said Clarice, her voice shaking. "Aren't these files open to anybody who wants to see them?"

"Yes, you little twit, they are. But, don't you remember? I told you not to ever let anybody back here unless I am in the office, too. Somebody needs to stay with them and make sure they don't try to alter any records or steal anything."

Clarice was pressed against the counter. She looked from me to her boss, her eyes pleading in my direction and filled with fear when they went toward her boss.

"Well, I didn't alter or steal anything," I said. I held out my hands. "As you can see, I brought nothing in with me but my car keys. Anyway, thank you, Clarice, I found out what company handled that land sale and I can tell my friend. Thank you, too," I said to the fat woman, Melinda Krupe, her name badge read. I felt a jolt when I realized what I was seeing. This must be Oliver Krupe's wife.

I felt her eyes like daggers in my back as I left the building. I strolled, trying to appear casual and unconcerned, although I wanted to run full speed up the street. I did a bit of window shopping in the boutique next door before I got into Blazer and drove away, the purloined papers crinkling against my back.

Back at Lola's I found Amy hard at work on her quilt. She had finished 18 nine-patch blocks and also cut out 17 plain color 6½ x 6½ inch blocks out of the lighter of the colors that she used in the nine patches. She was alternating them in seven rows of five blocks each. Because the solid blocks were the same color as the light color in the nine-patch blocks, that would leave the dark squares visually floating in rows across the middle of the quilt, creating a criss-cross pattern. She didn't even realize that she had just created a single Irish chain design in the center of her quilt, one of the oldest patterns around. I told her that if we got back to the fabric store in Long Beach we would look for Marti Michell's 101 Nine Patch Quilts book and I would show her the single Irish chain on page 30 called Not Scrap O' Nine Tales and the Irish chain variation on page 34. It was so much fun to see somebody else bitten by the quilting bug!

After we ate dinner I pulled out the papers I had copied at the town hall and showed them to Amy. "Do these look like your parents' signatures?"

Her eyes widened. "No, not a bit. My mom wrote in a straight up and down way and my dad had this lovely flowing way of signing his name. These don't even look close to their signatures. I just can't believe they are dead. There have been no bodies found anywhere. I checked all the funeral homes I could find today."

"But the signatures have been notarized," said Lola.

"Yeah, but look who the notary is," I said, pointing.

"My land," Lola said, "It's Melinda Krupe."

"Curiouser and curiouser, huh?"

"Who signed as the coroner?" asked Lola.

"I don't know. I can't read the writing," I said.

"What is going on, anyway?" Amy voice was shaking. "Did the sheriff kill my parents and hide the bodies? Is that why nobody can find them?"

"I don't know, Amy," I said. "But it sure appears that he is mixed up with Carl being able to get his hands on their property. As you can see by this," I said, handing her another of my copies, "Carl has since then sold the property. These are probably the fastest closings I have ever seen. He made a bundle, too. See where he bought the property for '$100 and thanks for all your hard work' and sold it for $50,000."

"I don't recognize the names of the buyers," Lola said. "They must not be local people."

"What can we do to find out?" Amy said.

"Lola, how honest is Glen Gunnison, do you know?"

Lola sat in thought for a minute. "As far as I know, he's okay. I have had to ask for his help a couple of times with the Rod Run people. You know how I turn my yard into a paid parking lot that weekend and occasionally some people get a little rowdy. He has always been happy to come and deal with them. Why?"

"Well, with that Krupe guy being the top dog there is really nobody to tell our suspicions to. I suppose I could try the state patrol or even the feds, but I'm not sure they would listen to us. The paper trail so far looks pretty convincing, but just to us. We really don't have any hard evidence, yet."

"But we have to do *something*," Amy wailed.

"We will," I said. "Lola, grab your phone book. Let's see if I can get lucky again and Glen Gunnison's address is in it."

He was the only Gunnison listed, gotta love these small towns. Talking to him would be my project for the next day. Right now, Amy and I had a quilt top to finish.

CHAPTER 29

▼

The next day was Saturday and the town would be full of weekenders. This would help, I could move around and not be so obvious as a stranger. After a quick breakfast, I put Henry in his harness and took him out on the beach. We would have a short walk before I set off to see if I could locate Glen Gunnison.

It was a windy day and lots of people were flying kites. Henry was entranced, staring up into the sky. I never knew a cat could stumble, but the sand was churned up from all the cars and people that had been over it. It would be hours before the tide came in and smoothed it all out. The second time Henry lost his footing I picked him up. I could see a piece of driftwood a ways up the beach. I would go sit down and he could watch the kites to his heart's content.

There was a bit of shelter from the wind here and it felt good to just sit in the sun and watch the people play. Henry swiveled his head around until I was sure he would have whiplash; so many kites to see. I liked to watch the people, especially those who it was obvious were making their first visit to a Washington beach. Dressed in bathing suits, they danced down the sand toward the water, some with a float toy in hand. Chasing the receding waves they would eagerly await the returning water. But when it hit them, that's when the fun really started.

Yes, this was the beach and the ocean. But, this far north the water really never got warm enough to spend any time in it. In fact, it was bone-chilling cold and feet would turn blue in a hurry, if the person could stand having them in the water even long enough to do that. I watched as both children and adults had their first experience with the cold Pacific Ocean. They retreated back up the beach, screeching and exclaiming, "BRRRRRRRRRRR, that's COLD." I enjoyed the drama. Henry ignored the screams; he had tested the water and he knew it was cold. Nobody would be able to laugh at him hollering about getting his feet frozen.

Feeling restless and not yet sure what I was going to say to Glen Gunnison once I found him, I decided to head back to Ilwaco and look around again for any sign of The Sea Ghost. Amy was sitting at my sewing machine, focused on matching seams and putting her quilt top together. She just nodded when I told her I was going to Ilwaco. I loaded Henry in his carrier and we took off.

Ilwaco was busy, lots of tourists in town. If Gary Wilson and his boat were taking people out on fishing trips this would be the time to find him and his boat. I put Henry's leash on him and we started toward the docks.

The surf was running a bit high, most of the smaller boats were in their slips. We walked up and down, but saw no sign of The Sea Ghost. I stopped at several slips to ask questions, but with the same results as on my previous search. Nobody knew anything about her or knew the name Gary Wilson. I finally gave up and stopped at a little sandwich shop and bought a turkey sub. I found a bench overlooking the water and sat and watched the big fishing boats work their way past the end of the jetty and out into the ocean.

I fed Henry bits of turkey from my sandwich and after it was gone I was ready to go back to Ocean Side. I wanted to go look for Glen Gunnison and Henry was bored. The boats no longer held his attention and he was pulling on his leash and bleating at me—it was time to leave.

The wastepaper can was over by the docks. I walked over to toss my sandwich wrappers and looked out to the jetty again, Henry tugging with impatience at his leash. There were kids playing on the rocks and dabbling their feet in the water, screaming the way kids always seem to do when they get around water. I dropped my trash and turned to go when something about the tone of the screams stopped me. While the oh-my-God-it's-cold screams were high-pitched and full of laughter, these sounded like shrieks of fear. I had heard screams like that just once before. A little boy fell in the pool at the gym at home where I swim and it had taken a few seconds to scoop him out. His mother's screams had been filled with terror. I felt the hair on the back of my neck stand up like it had on that day—this was something serious. Henry had quit pulling on his leash, too. He was standing rock still, staring out at the water.

"There's somebody out there, I can see them!" I heard a lady yell. "Somebody call 911!" another voice said. A man nearby pulled out his cell phone.

"It's no good, I can't get a signal," he said. He turned and ran toward the shore, yelling that he would find a phone.

I looked out where everybody was pointing. The jetty was formed from broken rock of all sizes that had been placed there in a long peninsula-like shape. It had been built to restrain the waves and currents from the ocean from washing back too far up the Columbia River and to protect the Ilwaco harbor and piers. It was not the sort of place where people went swimming, but there were nearly always fisherman there, their lines stretching out hopefully into the water. I could see a clump of people standing in one spot, pointing into the water on the side of the jetty away from me. I could not see what they were looking at.

After what seemed like an eternity, a sheriff's car came roaring onto the sand, pulling one of those funny Zodiac boats on a trailer. A man jumped out of the car wearing a wet suit. It was not anybody I recognized, but then I had had no contact with the Ilwaco police.

"Can somebody give me a hand here?" he yelled. A couple of men ran to his assistance and within seconds they had the boat in the water. The policeman started the small outboard and went bounding out across the water, the light Zodiac able to skim over the tops of the waves.

It only took a minute or two for him to get out to the jetty where the people were standing. I could see him pulling at something, then he clipped a line to his belt and jumped into the water. One of the men who had gone with him reached down and between the two of them they were able to load something that appeared large and ungainly into the boat. They turned around and headed back for the shore.

A tickle of fear crept up my back. I felt compelled to get as close to the action as I could; something was whispering to me that I was in some way involved with what was happening. Most of the people on the docks were standing and watching, too, wanting to know what happened as much as I did. I picked Henry up and held him close to my chest. His fur was all stickled up and he was making an unhappy humming noise deep in his throat. He didn't like trouble like this.

By the time I got to the beach on the far side of the jetty, the policeman had pulled the Zodiac up on the sand. Whatever he had pulled out of the water lay in the bottom of the boat, covered with a tarp.

"What is it?" I heard somebody ask.

"It's a woman," said the man who had gone with the policeman, "She's dead."

The crowd let out a collective moan and stepped back. I took the opportunity to step forward. I wanted to see. I had a bad feeling about this.

The policeman had gone to sit in his car and I could see that he was on the radio. Within minutes an ambulance pulled onto the sand, siren screaming. Two emergency medical technicians leaped out of the doors, grabbed a stretcher from the back, and ran over to where the mound lay in the bottom of the boat.

"No need to rush," I heard the policeman call out to the EMTs as he got out of his car, "She's been in the water a while."

"Who is it?" asked one of the EMTs.

"It looks like Clarice Miller," said the policeman. "She works up in Ocean Side. I don't have a positive ID yet, so I can't say for sure that's who it is."

Clarice. I felt my guts clench. That was the name of the clerk from the town hall who had helped me. I worked my way closer.

The EMTs set the stretcher down, then reached into the Zodiac for the tarp-covered bundle. They lifted it easily—this was not a big person. They set their load on the stretcher and a gust of wind blew the corner of the tarp away. I caught just a glimpse of the face before they were able to replace the cover. Yes. It was Clarice.

Feeling suddenly feeling sick to my stomach, I turned and ran back to the Blazer with Henry clinging to my shirt with all eighteen of his claws.

CHAPTER 30

▼

"…and I'm pretty sure it was the same girl that was working in the town hall that showed me those records and her boss is Melinda Krupe and she was really mad and Clarice was scared…oh, Lola." I was on my third cup of coffee and my teeth were still chattering.

"Hush, now," she said. "Try to calm down. People drown in the ocean, you know."

"Yes, but I felt like I sort of knew this girl. She was so willing to help me at the town hall and Melinda Krupe was so mean to her. Clarice was afraid of Melinda, I could tell."

"That doesn't surprise me," said Lola. "Melinda and that husband of her are two of a kind. They want their own way and nobody better cross them."

"Oh, God, Lola, you think Melinda *killed* Clarice? And if she did, it would be my fault." I couldn't stop my tears.

"Oh, I don't think she would go that far, Maggie. Clarice just may have swum out too far, or something."

"Lola! Even you know that couldn't be! Nobody actually swims off the jetty and that water is so cold that you can't stand to be in with for more than a few minutes without wearing a wet suit. Besides, it looked like she was dressed." Lola's talk therapy was working. My teeth had stopped chattering and I was beginning to feel my heart rate slow down. The days' events had gotten to Henry too. He was asleep on my bed with his paw over his eyes.

"I'm going to have to find out what happened," I said. "The police from Ilwaco pulled her out, and if it is Clarice from here maybe Glen Gunnison would know about it; this could be the opening I needed to talk to him and to get him to talk to me. I'll try and see him later."

Amy came out with her quilt's center panel all done. I was glad she had not heard any of Lola's and my conversation. More stress she did not need.

I took a deep breath and smiled as best I could. "Hey, you did a great job," I said. "Now all we have to do is put the frame and the outer border on and make the back. The back is easy to do, just one long seam."

"My corners aren't all exactly perfect," Amy said, pointing out the flaws.

"Don't worry about it, mine never are either. And as long as you don't point them out, nobody else will notice them. People will say, 'Oh, that's just perfect!' and you will feel compelled to say, 'No, look here, this is off and that is off.' Don't do that! Just take the praise, it feels good. Besides, I've pointed things out to people and they still say it's perfect, so so be it." I showed her how to do the frame piece of fabric and while she did that I helped Lola with dinner.

After we ate I spent a few more minutes showing Amy the next step in her quilt top, putting the border on. This followed the same steps at the frame, measure the length of the quilt and cut two strips the same length. Sew one to each side, then measure the quilt top from side to side. Cut two strips this width and sew them in place. Amy knew how to sew, so she could figure out how to cut out and put together the pieces of fabric for the back. I just told her to make sure her back was eight inches longer and wider than her finished top. "When I get ready to do the machine quilting I lay the back fabric out, then put the batting on top of it. The quilt top then goes on top of the batting and I pin all three layers together. While doing that the top stretches out some," I told her. "Then I could be in trouble, because the back will be too small if it's made exactly the same size as the top." This made sense to her and I left her to it.

Henry wasn't happy to stay behind, but I did not know what kind of a reception I would get at Glen Gunnison's house. I hadn't really figured out how to approach the deputy, as I wanted to talk to him away from his wife, if he had one. I feared a wagging tongue.

On the way up Glen's sidewalk inspiration hit. I knew just what to say. Now if he would just be the one to come to the door.

I was in luck. Glen Gunnison answered my knock.

"Hi, Glen, do you remember me? I'm Lola Bowen's niece. We met the night you came to her house."

"Yes, is it Maggie? What can I do for you?"

"Who is it, honey?" a voice called from in the house.

Quickly I said, "I have some information about the girl that drowned today."

He nodded. "It's somebody with some information for me," he replied. "We're going to go in the den." He held the door open and motioned me into a room that opened just off the front door.

"Have a seat," he said. "Can I get you anything? Coffee? I was just having some."

"That would be great, thanks."

While he was gone I looked around. This was obviously Glen's den. The furniture was dark wood with leather upholstery. The walls were covered in real knotty pine, no paneling here, and one whole wall was bookshelves from floor to ceiling. There were lots of interesting titles there and many of the books looked like antiques. I would like to have the time to do some browsing. This was such a rich-looking room, though. Was this another dirty cop? I was getting paranoid, for sure.

Deputy Gunnison came back carrying a tray. "I brought cream and sugar, too," he said, "I wasn't sure how you like your coffee."

"Thank you, Deputy Gunnison. I do like to use cream and sugar occasionally as a treat—it's almost like dessert. This is a great den."

"Yes, it is, isn't it. After my parents moved south they sold us their house. This was my dad's favorite room and I always liked it, too. It's the one place we didn't redecorate after we moved in." He picked up his coffee cup and took a drink.

After we sipped for a minute, he said, "You said something about having some information about the girl that was found in the ocean today?"

"I might have, depending on how she died. Did she drown?"

Deputy Gunnison squirmed in his chair. "I don't know that I am at liberty to say. Why do you want to know, anyway?"

This would be the tough part. If he was in cahoots with Oliver Krupe this could be the end of anything I could do to help Amy, or get justice for Clarice, either. I had no choice but to go for it.

"Well," I said, "I don't know exactly where to start, so I guess at the beginning. I came to Ocean Side a week or so ago to teach a class at the quilt camp being run by the Ocean View Quilters club at the Seacoast Inn. The Washington Longarm Guild is having their annual meeting and I wanted to take a few classes. The Ocean View club is sponsoring the Longarm Guild meeting and they asked me to come do a class on beginning quilting for them. As you already know, my aunt, Lola Bowen, lives in Ocean Side and I am staying with her.

"One day I went into Lucille's Beach House, which used to belong to Lola and her husband, and I got to talking to Amy Sanders."

Deputy Gunnison opened his mouth, but I held up my hand. "Wait just a minute. I know you think you know all about that, but maybe you don't."

I went on to tell him again everything I knew about Amy and the search for her parents. Deputy Gunnison looked bored, this was nothing he hadn't already heard. But, he sat up straighter in his chair and looked intently at me when I said, "So, we went to Ilwaco to talk to this Gary Wilson, but neither he nor his supposed boat, The Sea Ghost, apt name, don't you think? seem to exist. And, Sheriff Krupe's behavior has seemed so callous and uncaring toward Amy. He just won't listen to her when she says her parents are missing, not dead."

"But, that can't be right," said Glen. "I saw the death certificates myself stating drowning as a cause of death of Bethel and George Armstrong and I read the accident report. And, I can't really blame Ollie, he likes me to call him that, for brushing off Amy. She just wouldn't listen to him when he told her that her parents had moved away. He just heard about their drowning and told me he hasn't yet had a chance to talk to Amy."

"Excuse me, Deputy Gunnison, but that's bullshit. Take another look at the dates on those certificates. Your 'Ollie' has known since the day they supposedly drowned what happened and that was the same day Amy arrived here, weeks ago. And are you sure those certificates are genuine? Can you read the coroner's name? And what about the signatures on the land sale papers that Amy said are not legitimate, either?"

"Yes, I suppose I need to talk to her again. Now, what does all this have to do with today's death?"

"That was a young woman named Clarice who was found, right?"

Deputy Gunnison sighed. "I suppose it's okay to verify that."

I let my head drop. I had known, but still the official confirmation was a blow. "And did she drown, Deputy Gunnison?"

"Please call me Glen, Maggie. All that 'deputy' stuff gets a little wearing."

A little knot of tension inside me loosened. If he was willing to forgo his title and be just a guy, maybe he was honest after all.

He sighed again. "One of the deputies in Ilwaco is a friend of mine. Once they figured out who she was, he called and told me what they had discovered. There was no water in her lungs when they did the autopsy and there was a question of her hyoid bone being broken."

"So, she was dead when she went into the water and it sounds like somebody strangled her first, right?"

He stared at me. "You watch a lot of medical shows on TV, right?"

I had to laugh. "Yes, and 'COPS' too. No, actually, I'm an RN and I read a lot of mystery and police procedural books, besides. I know how fragile that hyoid bone in the neck is and how it is often broken when somebody is choked. So, knowing that, now I have to tell you that her death may be my fault."

"How could that be?" he asked. "You didn't even know her, did you?"

"Well, not really. Remember those land sale papers I showed you? I got those from the files at the town hall, they are copies, actually."

"That's not a problem, such paperwork in part of the Freedom of Information Act and open for public perusal," he said, "Although I'm surprised you were able to get copies."

I pretended I hadn't heard what he said about the copies, hoping he would just assume they had been given to me. I did not want Melinda Krupe to know I had them.

"Just after Clarice showed me the files, her boss showed up. She accused me of being there to alter the papers and was very angry at Clarice. Clarice looked scared of her, too."

"And Clarice's boss was Melinda Krupe." Glen had figured it out for himself. "I have heard stories about her; she can be quite a hellcat. Are you accusing Melinda of killing Clarice, though? That's a pretty serious thing to suggest."

Now it was time to fish or cut bait, as they say around these parts. If Glen Gunnison was tangled up in any deals with Oliver Krupe, my goose was cooked. I thought for a minute, not really sure what to say first. Might as well jump in with both feet, I decided.

"I'm wondering if your Ollie is crooked," I said, and watched Glen's face. I saw his mouth sag and he turned to stare out the window.

"All I ever wanted to be was a good cop," he said. "I was deputy under Mike Thompson and hoped some day to follow in his footsteps. He was a great guy, honest as the day is long. He would sooner starve than accept a bribe or take any-thing that he didn't earn. But, I was still just a greenhorn when he died. Folks didn't think I would be up to handling the sheriff's job. Oliver Krupe had moved here from the east side of the state and took on a few hours as a part-time deputy. After Mike died, Oliver was able to razzle-dazzle the voters with all his 'big city' knowledge. He won the election and became sheriff.

"At first I thought he was going to be okay. But, one day I had to call for backup when I had pulled over a car that I was pretty sure had drugs hidden in it. He came and helped me secure the two guys, then we searched the car.

"Sure enough, there was marijuana hidden under the floor of the trunk. We also found a packet of money hidden in the bottom of the back seat. Now, I'm not a banker, but I do know that $1000 in $100 dollar bills does not make a very thick stack. We fanned through at least twenty-five stacks of bills, and they were all $100s."

I could see where this was going and I almost jumped in and finished the story for him. But, I didn't want to distract him, so I sat quietly and waited.

"When we got back to the office, Oliver sent me back into the jail area to secure our suspects while he started the paperwork. He said that I already had seen the drugs and the money, so to save time he would just seal up the evidence box while I was busy in the cell area. The procedure was that after putting the marijuana and the money in the evidence box he would seal it shut. Then he would put an inventory list on the top to establish the chain of evidence that proves that whatever we had recovered from the car had been constantly in the sight of one of us. Then, together we would lock it up in the office safe until the case was ready to go to trial. We didn't want the bad guys to later say we had planted anything on them or among their belongings.

"I got done before he expected me to, I guess, because he left the box sitting by his desk while he ran across the street for donuts. It was all sealed up and the list was on the top, just like it was supposed to be. Except, he had put down $10,000 in cash recovered. My guess is that he had held out about $15,000."

"What did you do?"

Glen shook his head. "Nothing, and that makes me no better than he. When I saw him coming back from the bakery I ducked back to the cell area. I pretended to just be coming out for the first time when he walked in. I wanted to ask him if he took the money, but I wasn't totally positive that he had. I knew he held my future in his hands and I didn't want to risk losing it. After all, we hadn't really sat down on the roadside and counted the money, maybe some of those packets held smaller bills. So, I just signed on the label as to what was inside and tried to forget about it. But, I never have been able to."

"I think you were right about that and I also think that now he's branched out," I said. "He has a house on the bay with a fancy speed boat tied to the dock and my aunt says he has a valuable antique car."

"But what does that have to do with Amy Sanders and her parents?"

"I think Carl Rolley is part of all this, too. Lola tells me that Carl can do no wrong as far as the sheriff is concerned and that Oliver uses him as his personal handyman. I'm not really sure how it all came about, but I think that Carl had a hand in the disappearance of Amy parents. Then, with Oliver helping him, and I bet that his wife Melinda is involved too, she would have access to all sorts of official forms and documents in her job at the town hall, Carl was able to sell all the Armstrong's things. Then Carl split the money with Oliver. Now I wonder if Melinda is worried that I saw something in those papers I shouldn't have. Clarice was helping me and Melinda may have thought that I said something to her and then she knew about it, too, whatever it was. Clarice may have been killed to ensure her silence; which makes me real nervous for me, my aunt, and Amy."

Glen looked sick to his stomach. He pushed his coffee cup aside. "I have wondered for a long time how Ollie manages to spend the way he does; I know what his salary is."

"Now the question is, Glen, what can we do about this?"

"I guess the place to start would be with the Armstrongs. I will see if I can locate this Gary Wilson guy, he may have just been an itinerant fisherman who called himself a charter operator and took the Armstrongs out just for the money with no intention of doing any fishing. There has been some trouble with that happening in the past. Ilwaco requires any charter boat to be licensed and safety checked before they are allowed to advertise for paying customers, but there is always some guy looking to make a quick buck. If the Armstrongs did go out The Sea Ghost and drown, the boat owner probably left the area as soon as he could. There should be boat registration numbers recorded in the file somewhere; I'll check on it as soon as I can."

"Be careful, Glen. I'm getting scared of this Krupe pair, they sound ruthless."

I left him sitting at his desk, staring into his empty coffee cup.

CHAPTER 31

▼

Lola's house was dark and quiet by the time I got back. I hadn't realized it was so late, she and Amy had already gone to bed.

Henry was up, though, and greeted me with glad meows. I picked him up and he pulled himself up so he could stick his nose in my ear and purr. I let him do this for a minute, even though it gave me the shivers. Then I took him out to the kitchen and put some dry food in his bowl.

While he crunched, I paced. I was too restless to sleep, but I didn't want to wake Amy or Lola. I finally decided to check my email, maybe Rick had gotten some answers from Marty.

Henry came and sat next to my laptop. He loved all the little noises it made and the way things flashed off and on the screen. Every now and then he would reach out a curious paw and touch the screen. As soon as I got to AOL and my mailbox, though, he went over and curled up on the bed. It's like he knew there wouldn't be much screen action for awhile.

There was the usual spam, did I want a bigger penis? How about refinancing my mortgage? Viagra by mail! Women with farm animals, UG. That's what the delete key is for, it all went into the trash, unopened. But, there was a note from Rick and also one from an address I hadn't seen before, but that I was sure was not more spam. Copmarty was the name.

Rick's note said that Cleo and Marmalade, the two lady cats, and Brandy, the Greyhound, were all doing well. He said that Sully was spending a lot of time with them and they didn't seem too lonely. At least these guys would eat if I left home, Henry wouldn't, which was why I had to haul him around with me. He also said that he had forwarded my email to Marty and given him my email address. He said he hoped that was okay. His 'I love you' at the end warmed my heart.

Marty's mail was interesting, too, although without a lot of real information. He said that he had been able to get hold of originals of the Armstrong's death certificates and that he had passed them on to the documents division to see if they were authentic. He had also started a trace on the GEO Metro that the Armstrongs had owned and was looking for the paperwork on the sale of the truck. He hoped to have some answers for me soon.

I sent him back the names of Susan and Dan Carson as the buyers of the truck and asked him to do a background check on Carl Rolley, too. I didn't know how much of this he could do, after all, Pacific County was just a little outside his jurisdiction in Spokane County.

I remembered what it had been like when Rick and I were trying to uncover Lynda Mancusco's part in the drug smuggling in the vet clinic where he and I worked. Rick had written everything down and put the statement in his safety deposit box so that if anything happened to either him or me, the authorities would know where to start an investigation.

Now that sounded like a good idea to me, too. I spent the next couple of hours writing down everything I could think of that had to do with Amy, Oliver Krupe, the Armstrongs, Carl Rolley, everything. I hadn't brought my printer with me, but I put in all on a floppy disk. I wrapped the disk in several layers of paper and addressed it to Rick. I enclosed a note telling him what it was all about; he would know what to do with it, should a situation arise.

I slipped out of the house and went to the post office and put the disk in the outgoing box. I didn't feel any safer, but I knew if anything happened to me or any of the rest of us there would be an investigation.

By the time I got back to Lola's I was ready for sleep.

CHAPTER 32

▼

Lola put our breakfast dishes in the dishwasher and told me she was going to go to the Costco that was just across the river in Oregon. She needed nuts for the squirrels, she said. I didn't laugh at her, that wouldn't be fair. I bought a fair amount of peanuts at our Costco for my squirrels and chipmunks at home. Amy decided to go with her, hoping the change of scene would help her mood. Now that the distraction the making of her quilt top had provided was gone, the stress of her parents' disappearance was weighing on her again.

I took Henry out on the beach and we walked for over an hour. He was begging to be carried by the time we got back to Lola's house. I took him in and settled him down on the bed.

I didn't really know what to do next. Finally I decided to drive by the Armstrong's trailer site again. Henry was asleep and didn't even move when I rattled the cat carrier, so I left him to his nap.

Before I went out to the Blazer I picked up Lola's morning paper. I turned to the obituaries and saw that Clarice's funeral was scheduled for Monday afternoon. I wouldn't go; I hadn't really known her and I was supposed to be back in Spokane by then, but I felt a need to go and see her parents. I read that they only lived two houses down the street from Lola, so I decide to walk to their house before I went by the Armstrongs' place again.

I went up the sidewalk and onto the porch of a cottage painted a soft blue. Taking a deep breath, I tapped on the door. A red-eyed woman answered my knock.

"Hello, Mrs. Miller? My name is Maggie Jackson and I just wanted to say how sorry I was to hear about Clarice."

She held the door open wider. "You knew Clarice? Won't you come in?"

I stepped into a living room decorated in shades of blue. There were several floral bouquets placed about and I saw the one I had sent to them with the collection on the piano.

"This is Clarice's father, Stuart. Stuart, this is a friend of Clarice's, what did you say your name was, again?"

"Maggie Jackson, it is nice to meet you, Mr. Miller, and I am so sorry about Clarice."

He reached out to shake my hand. "I don't remember my daughter mentioning you. Had you known her for very long?"

"No, Mr. Miller. I'm in town visiting and actually just met her a few days ago. She helped me get some information down at the town hall."

"She was good at her job, but that was just a stepping stone for her. She was going to be working for a big corporation some day," he said.

"But that woman took care of that," Clarice's mother said. "I just know she had something to do with Clarice's death. Clarice would not have tried to swim off the jetty like the sheriff said. She knew better than that."

"Now, mother, you can't be saying that just because Clarice didn't like her boss very well…"

Mrs. Miller interrupted him. "It was more than that, Stu, you know that." She turned to me. "Clarice told me lots of times that she was really afraid of Melinda Krupe. She said Melinda threatened her if she ever made a mistake or did anything that Melinda didn't like."

"I did hear Melinda giving Clarice a bit of a hard time when I was in the office," I said, "But she didn't seem to be threatening her."

"That's probably because you were there. That Melinda is an evil woman."

Mr. Miller started to fidget in his chair. "We need to be careful, Mary. Melinda is the sheriff's wife, you know."

It was time for me to go. I had expressed my condolences and I did not want to intrude on their grief. But, they obviously did not like Melinda Krupe and I wanted to know more.

"It seems a lot of people around here are worried about the sheriff. Do you know why?"

The Millers looked at each other. Mr. Miller shook his head, but Mrs. Miller said, "He's not a nice man. If you try to object to anything he does you start having all kinds of bad luck. He pulls you over and gives you a ticket for any little

thing. There has also been some talk about him killing a dog that barked at him."
She shivered. "I'm afraid of him. And to think that his awful wife killed my baby.
She was our only child, you know."

"He won't even tell us what happened to her," said Stuart Miller. "He keeps
telling us that she fell while trying to climb those rocks, or went swimming off
the jetty, but I don't believe him. Do you know what happened?"

I didn't think Deputy Gunnison would like it if I told the Millers what he had
told me. But, maybe he would be willing to talk to them. "No, I really don't. But,
Deputy Gunnison knows the Ilwaco policeman who was on the beach when she
was found. You might try talking to him."

"Thank you," said Mr. Miller. "We'll do that."

I had overstayed my welcome by now. "I better get going. Again, I am so sorry
about your daughter."

I walked back to Lola's and went in to lie down on my bed; the trip to the
Armstrongs' place would have to wait. I felt nauseated by the grief I had encoun-
tered at the Millers. While there was no way I could tell how they really felt, I had
some idea. The pain and depression that I had to struggle through following the
loss of my unborn baby had almost been overwhelming. I couldn't imagine what
it would be like to lose a child that you had come to know and love as a person in
their own right. Phil Scott and his partner in crime, Norm, had robbed me of
that chance. Their brutal assault had cut short my baby's life five months before
its birth. While I might forgive Phil for his criminal behavior and the death of
our marriage, my baby's death I could never forgive. I just hoped he and Norm
were both suffering in many ways while they sat in prison.

Lola and Amy were not back yet and the house seemed to be pressing in on
me. Henry was not interested in going with me after our long walk this morning,
but I had to get out. I headed for the beach.

I walked until I felt the pain inside starting to ease, then headed back to the
house. I would surprise Lola and start our dinner.

I was chilled by the wind coming off the water, so I decided to walk up the
street on my way back to the house. As I came closer I saw a car I didn't recognize
parked in the driveway. But then, I certainly didn't know all of Lola's friends or
what kind of cars they drove. I started up the driveway and I was just passing a
large rhododendron bush when the front door flew open. Two men came charging across the porch and down the driveway toward me. It was Carl Rolley and

Oliver Krupe. I threw myself onto the ground and slithered as far under the bush as I could. I put my head down on my arms and hoped they wouldn't see me.

"Rawr, moohoo, psssst, ik, ik, ik, meYOW." I jerked my head up and saw Henry come out the door, running after the men. Black paws tipped with gleaming white claws slashed in front of him as he ran, his yowls and shrieks splitting the air.

"Goddamn, Goddamn, what the hell is that?" yelled Carl. "Get the hell out of my way, man."

Carl pushed at Oliver and stumbled past him. Oliver skidded to a stop, turned, drew his gun, and fired, all in one motion.

Henry let out a bloodcurdling screech and flew into the air. He landed on the gravel with a sickening thud, his tongue hanging out the side of his mouth. I could see a trickle of red running down his side. I clamped my hands over my mouth to stifle my own screams.

Henry was dead. I knew it. There was no way his fragile little body could survive a gun shot. These men would not hesitate to kill me, too, if they knew I had seen what they did. But, I would avenge Henry; Oliver Krupe would pay. Hot tears began to flow down my face and I fought not to sob out loud.

"You said no guns, asshole!" yelled Carl.

"What are you going to do, call the cops?" snarled Oliver Krupe. They jumped into the car in the driveway and roared away.

I crawled out from under the bush the moment their car was out of sight. I needed to go to Henry, but I could not make myself stand up and walk over to him. I crouched on my hands and knees by the bush crying out loud, my tears soaking the ground. Finally, I was able catch my breath and get my feet under me.

Choking and gasping for air, I staggered over to Henry's body. How could I have let this happen? How would I go on without my kitty? He had been with me through everything, first the joy of my marriage to Phil, then all the dreadful times of the assault, the miscarriage, the embezzlement discovery, the trial, and the divorce.

Henry had crawled into my arms at every opportunity after Phil had been taken away. He kissed me on the nose and nuzzled my ears, purring as loud as he could. This had been new behavior for him then; it was like he understood my misery. He had given me a reason to get up in the morning and he was the only thing in my life during that time that could make me smile.

I dropped down onto the gravel and reached out for Henry, but before I could touch his fur he lifted his head up and looked around. He glanced at me, but then took a long searching look down the driveway. He carefully stood up and shook himself, then winced and licked at his shoulder.

My head spun and for a moment I had to sit and concentrate on remaining conscious. "Henry, my God, you're not dead. Oh, kitty, please don't move around any more, you've been shot." I struggled to my feet and reached for him.

He ignored me and kept trying to lick at his shoulder. Then he turned and walked back to the house, limping slightly on his front paw. My legs were rubbery and felt useless, but I managed to lurch my way up the driveway and pick him up. There was a soft spongy area on his shoulder—that must have been where the bullet hit him. I needed to get him to a vet, right now.

I went into the house, put Henry in his carrier and ran for the phone book. My hands were shaking so hard I could scarcely turn the pages.

"Ocean Side Animal Hospital," the voice on the phone said.

For a minute I couldn't even talk, I was so relieved to have my call answered. "My cat just got shot," I was finally able to gasp. "I need to bring him in to get checked out. Can we come right over?" My voice wasn't shaking too badly, I was glad to note.

"Yes, by all means," the clinic receptionist said. "You know where we are located?"

She gave me directions and I ran for the Blazer, Henry's carrier swinging from my hand.

Jack Cannen was the veterinarian. He knew Brad Mancusco, and while he had talked to Rick on the phone, they had never met. It helped, though. I almost felt like I was home in the All Animals Hospital in Spokane.

Henry stood rock-still on the examination table while Dr. Cannen examined him. "I need to do some x-rays, Henry. Are you going to let me do that?"

Henry gazed up at him and bobbed his head. "Looks like he will," said Dr. Cannen. "We'll be right back."

Within minutes they were back. He set Henry on the table then went back for the films. While I waited I picked Henry up and stroked his head. He squinted his eyes at me and purred, his front paws kneading the air.

Dr. Cannen came back and clipped the x-ray pictures on the light box. "It looks like Henry got lucky, Maggie. Look here," he said, pointing at the x-ray. "That bullet must have just grazed his shoulder. I don't see any sign of anything foreign in his shoulder and no broken bones. He's going to be fine. I'll just need to clip some fur away from that wound so I can see if he needs stitches. I'll need to give him just a touch of Ketamine so he won't feel what we are doing."

Henry seemed to be in a trance. He watched Dr. Cannen calmly as he clipped away a square of fur on his front leg and felt for a vein. I was impressed by the ease in which he was able to slip a small needle into Henry's vein. He injected a small amount of medication and Henry's body went limp.

"He'll only sleep for a few minutes, so I'll need to work fast." Dr. Cannen said. He grabbed the clippers he had used to expose the IV site and started to work on Henry's shoulder. Soon there was bare skin on both sides of a shallow furrow.

"Just like I thought," he said. "It's just a skin wound. Look here. The bullet must have just grazed him; taking off a swath of skin and fur. There isn't even anything that needs stitches, but it may ooze for a while. Don't be alarmed if it does."

Henry was starting to paddle with his front paws. "He's waking back up, good," said Dr. Cannen. "You can take him home, but remember, their bodies recover from that drug from the head down, so his back legs won't work too well for awhile. It'd be best to leave him in his carrier until he can stand up." Dr. Cannen gave Henry a shot of penicillin to ward off any infection then applied an antibiotic ointment on the scraped skin. He handed me the tube.

"Use this twice a day for about a week then let the wound dry up. If there are any problems give me a call. Rick Evans can take over any other care Henry needs when you get home."

"That won't be hard to do," I said, "At least this is in a spot where he can't reach to lick it and the ointment will stay on." I couldn't stop the explosion of giggles that erupted. I laughed until I was weeping, embarrassing myself, but unable to stop.

Dr. Cannen looked at me for a minute. "Are you going to be all right?"

I took a deep breath. "Yes, it has just been a hell of a day, that's all," I said, mopping my streaming eyes. "I came to Ocean Side to teach a quilt class and you wouldn't believe all the stuff that has happened. I just lost it there for a minute when I realized that Henry is going to be okay."

"You have me worried, Maggie," said the vet.

Henry looked up at me with glazed eyes. "He should be fine," said Dr. Cannen as he helped me slide Henry into his carrier. Henry looked up at me with a pathetic silent meow, then put his head down and closed his eyes. "Looks like he's going to nap. Now, Maggie, what happened today anyway? You know I should report this as a gunshot wound."

"Don't bother, Dr. Cannen. It was the sheriff who shot him."

"What? Why would the sheriff do that?"

"I'm not exactly sure what they were up to, but Sheriff Krupe and Carl Rolley were in my aunt's house where I am staying. Lola Bowen's place? Do you know her?"

Dr. Cannen nodded.

"I got home just in time to see Henry chase them out the front door. The sheriff turned and shot at him as he and Carl were running away." I could feel the giggles bubbling up again and clenched my jaw to still them.

"They were in your aunt's house? Was she home?"

"No, there was nobody home when I went in to call you, thank goodness."

Dr. Cannen stood and looked at me for a minute. "Our sheriff can be a bit hot-headed at times, but why would he break into your aunt's house?"

"I don't know," I said, "But it's possible he was looking for some information I have gathered. I have gotten to know a young woman, Amy Sanders, who came here to visit her parents and found them gone. She has been trying to find out what happened to them and has gotten nothing but rebuffs from the Sheriff. I was starting to think that Krupe was involved, and now, after what happened today, I'm sure of it."

"In what way?" asked Dr. Cannen.

"I'm not really sure yet, but I think Krupe either had something to do with Amy's parents disappearance or he knows who did. At first he was trying to make everybody believe that they just moved away. Now he is saying that they drowned in a boating accident, but too many things just don't add up. I think money is at the bottom of everything. Now I have to try and figure out how to expose Krupe and his partners in crime."

Dr. Cannen looked at Henry, asleep in his carrier. "You need to be careful, Maggie. If Sheriff Krupe is mixed up in anything like this and if he would shoot a cat he would probably do anything to prevent anybody from finding out what he is doing."

"I know. It's a little scary. But, I have a deputy sheriff friend in Spokane who is checking on things for me and he knows the whole story. If anything were to happen to me I know he'd step in. Well, I better get this cat of mine home. What do I owe you?"

I wrote Dr. Cannen a check and drove back to Lola's. Henry slept the whole way.

CHAPTER 33

▼

When I got back to Lola's and took Henry out of his carrier his back legs were a little unsteady, but they would hold him up. I left him eating some Deli Cat and went to check things in the house. Everything seemed to be undisturbed in the living room, kitchen, dining room, and Lola and Amy's rooms. But, my room was a nightmare. I was just starting to look around in there when I heard Lola and Amy come in.

"Henry," I heard Lola say, "What on earth happened to you?"

"It's a long story, Lola," I called out to her. "If you want to put the coffee on, I'll straighten up in here and come and tell you about it."

From the condition of the room, Henry must have scared Oliver and Carl away before they could finish searching it. The dresser drawers and closet had been emptied, the contents were all over the floor, but my sewing boxes and suitcase full of fabric were not disturbed. They also had not found what I was sure they were looking for, the copies of the papers I had gotten at the town hall. I would bet by now the originals were gone from the files where I had found them. I knew they didn't have the papers because I had stuck them in the bottom of a fabric box and it was undisturbed. Good job, Henry! I scooped up all my clothes and other possessions and dumped them on the bed. I would sort things out later. I went out to tell Lola and Amy what had gone on.

"So, Henry ended up chasing Oliver and Carl out of the house and he almost got shot to death in the process. But, I don't know what to do. It's not like we can call the cops for help, that's for sure."

"What about that detective you told me about you know in Spokane?" said Amy.

"Yeah, he's checking on some things for me. Next time I talk to him I'll tell him all the rest of this stuff and see what he says. In the meantime, Lola, you better start locking your doors."

"Yes, I suppose I must," she said, looking troubled.

"One good thing did come of this, though," I said. "Now I am positive that the sheriff is involved whatever happened to Amy's parents."

"How do you know that?"

"Well, I'm sure Melinda told her husband about seeing me at the town hall. He probably suspects I took papers. Besides, I told Glen Gunnison about the copies I had and he may have said something to Oliver, too."

Lola went to the door and turned the key in the dead bolt. "There," she said, "That should slow down anybody who tries to get in here."

CHAPTER 34

▼

The next day there was another email from Marty. He wrote and told me that the death certificates were genuine, to a point. The forms were authentic, he said, but the information had not been entered in the usual fashion. Usually these forms were printed from a computer printer, he wrote, where these had been filled out using a typewriter. He said that it was the kind of typewriter that uses a single-use ribbon, and that if the typewriter could be found and if the same ribbon was still in place, all the information that had been typed on the death certificates could be read off the ribbon. That might indicate if the certificates had been filled out by the correct office.

The coroner's signature was a totally unreadable scribble. Marty said it looked like somebody was trying to make it look like a doctor's way of signing his name, but that the experts at the Spokane County Sheriff's department had not been able to make out any sort of name. He said that was another reason the certificates were suspect.

The GEO Metro and the Chevy truck titles had been properly transferred after supposedly being sold by the Armstrongs. But, again the signatures did not look right for the Armstrongs, he said. The handwriting expert had pointed out several places where the person signing hesitated, almost like they didn't know how to spell the names. He said he did not think the signatures were genuine, but that he would need samples of the Armstrongs' handwriting to be sure. Marty was unable to find any information on the trailer, as I had no VIN or any other kind of identifying numbers to give him.

He also had not been able to come up with any information about a boat captain named Gary Wilson or a boat called The Sea Ghost. This did not surprise me, I had already decided this man and his boat were figments of somebody's imagination.

I felt at a loss. I really didn't know what direction to go in next. I was sitting and staring out the window, trying to come up with a plan, or just an idea, bright or not. I jumped when Amy walked in; I had been a thousand miles away.

"Hi, Maggie, sorry to scare you. I was wondering, could we go look around at the place where my parents had their trailer?"

"Sure, we can do that. I was actually thinking about doing that yesterday, but Henry getting shot made me forget my plans. What are you hoping to see there?"

"I don't know," she said. "I just feel like I need to see the spot again."

"Here we are," I said a few minutes later. Amy got out and walked over to the now-vacant lot. I let her be, she seemed to need the time alone. I looked around, too, but all was quiet. None of the other neighbors were anywhere to be seen.

Amy got back in the Blazer. "Thanks for bringing me here, Maggie. I feel better now," she said, wiping tears from her cheeks. "I somehow feel close to mom and dad here. I know how much they loved living here. I just wish I knew what had happened to them."

"I heard from my sheriff friend in Spokane this morning," I said. "He told me that the signatures look fake on the car and truck titles, but that the titles were transferred to the new owners legally, or so it appears. The Carsons have the truck, and guess what, our friend Carl Rolley is shown as the new owner of the GEO Metro."

"Then we know that he stole the car, don't we?"

"Well, not exactly. Just knowing that the signatures might be fake could be kind of dead end. Your folks would have to be the ones saying that the signatures aren't theirs, and as far as the law is concerned, they are dead, drowned."

Amy's tears were gone, now she looked furious. "But we know that isn't true! That man and his boat don't even exist."

"I agree with you, but that will be hard to prove, too. Down in Ilwaco they said they have a certain number of itinerant fisherman that come and go without leaving a trace behind them. Sometimes they fall into a conversation with a tourist and offer a fishing trip for a cash payment. It's possible that's what happened with your parents. And, of course the problem is that we would need Oliver Krupe to ask the police in Ilwaco to look into it and I don't think we can convince him to do anything. I am convinced he's tangled up in all this somehow." I didn't share with her my feelings that he was in league with Carl Rolley.

"But there might be a way to prove the death certificates were fake. Marty, my cop friend from Spokane said that they were typed rather than run from a computer printer. Now we have to figure out how to get hold of the ribbon from the town hall office to see if that's where those certificates were typed. I would be willing to bet that Oliver Krupe has his wife involved in all this, too. I noticed her driving around in an Audi and they don't come cheap. And as far as those signatures are concerned, it just occurred to me that if you know of any documents with your parents signatures on them that have been notarized—that could help prove the signatures on the car and truck titles and the land sale papers are fakes."

Amy nodded her head. "Yes, I'm pretty sure I know where my mother kept all that stuff. She and I share a safety deposit box back home. I bet the paperwork is there for the purchase and sale of the apartment; and those would have notarized signatures. I don't think she took them out before they moved. I could probably get them, if I needed to."

"That's good, Amy. That probably would work. We better get moving; we've been sitting here awhile and I think the neighbors are going to start to wonder," I said, seeing a curtain move in the Olsen sisters' house. "Do you want to run up to Oysterville and get some more oysters? You seemed to like them pretty well the other night."

"Okay," said Amy, "I guess that would be good."

She sat quietly on our way up the peninsula, just staring out the car window. We were almost to the oyster packing plant when she let out a shout.

"Stop, oh, Maggie, stop! There's the trailer; I see my mom and dad's trailer." Amy was pointing wildly out the window. I pulled over and almost before the Blazer had stopped moving she had jumped out and was running across the grass in front of a large mobile home.

"Mom! Dad!" She yelled as she ran. The door of the trailer opened and a young woman with a baby on her hip stepped out. Amy stopped short, then walked up to the trailer. I could see her and the young woman talking, then Amy turned back my way. Her shoulders drooped and she moved across the grass in slow motion.

"That was not my mom," she said, "But I guess you could tell that."

"Are you sure this is the same trailer?"

"Yes. See that watermelon painted on the end there?" she said, pointing. "My mom loved watermelon and an artist friend of hers painted this on the trailer as a going away present. My mom had sent me a picture. I can show it to you, it's in my stuff at your aunt's house. That lady said they bought the trailer at the same time they bought their piece of property here."

This was something else I could now ask Marty to check for me. I knew that there was a VIN type of number on a mobile home. I grabbed a piece of paper and a pen and slipped out of Blazer and went up to the end where the watermelon was painted. Yes. There was a tag riveted to the body of the trailer. I quickly copied down the number and the trailer manufacturer's name and ran back to the Blazer.

"Let's get out of here. I don't to want make anybody suspicious," I said. "We'll go get those oysters then we'll go back to Lola's. I'll send this info to Marty as soon as we get there.

CHAPTER 35

▼

That night I lay in bed, trying to figure out what to do. Somehow I needed to get my hands on the typewriter ribbon from the town hall to see if it showed that the Armstrong's death certificates had been typed on it. But, Melinda Krupe knew who I was by now. I knew she would watch me like a hawk if I showed up in the town hall again. Also, I didn't want to take a chance on anybody else getting hurt. If Clarice died because she helped me…I felt a clutch in my stomach that I may have caused this young woman's death. I wouldn't risk asking anything from any other town hall clerk. If only we really knew where Amy's parents were. With that thought in mind, I drifted off to sleep.

The next morning my brain was still spinning about the typewriter ribbon. Maybe that should be my next step.

"Lola, how would you like to play detective?" I asked her over our breakfast coffee.

"That depends. Am I going to get shot like Henry was?"

"I don't think so. I've been pondering how to get hold of the typewriter ribbon from the town hall. If we can figure out what kind of typewriter it is and if I can get another ribbon, maybe I can also figure out how to take the one that is in there and put the new one in."

"What on earth do you need that for?" Lola asked.

"Marty Adams told me that Amy's parents' death certificates were typed, rather than the forms being run through a computer printer like they usually are. He said that the information should show on the ribbon itself. Marty said the documents people that looked at the certificates could tell that they had been typed on the kind of typewriter that uses a ribbon that is single use. The ink is on a strip of plastic and as you type, the ink is transferred off the plastic and onto the paper. You can read what has been typed by unrolling the ribbon and holding it up to the light. If the information on the death certificates was typed with the Ocean Side Town Hall typewriter, that would be unusual, as the certificates usually come from the county seat. This might get the State Patrol or even the FBI interested in the Armstrong's disappearance."

"Oh, Maggie, I don't think I would be brave enough to try and switch typewriter ribbons," said Lola, frowning.

"And I don't want you to try," I said. "But, if you could find out what kind of typewriter they have, then I could get a ribbon and figure out a way to swap them. What do you think—do you want to try it?"

Lola swirled the last of the coffee in her cup then tossed it into her mouth. "Why not?" she said. "I'll do it today." She got up and left the kitchen, looking determined.

Amy had listened to us without saying anything. She turned to me and said, "If Lola can figure out about the typewriter and all that, how are we going to get the old ribbon out and the new one in?"

"That part I haven't figured out yet. Let's see if Lola can get the info for us, first."

Henry and I went for a walk on the beach, then I helped Amy put the last finishing touches on her quilt top. She had arranged her nine-patch squares into a single Irish chain design after all, one of the oldest and most popular quilt patterns. I was so proud of her; she had done a marvelous job for her first attempt.

"I'll take this home with me and quilt it for you," I told her. "Just give me your address and I'll send it to you."

I went back out and paced up and down the beach behind Lola's house, worried about her. She had been gone for a couple of hours and knowing that Ollie Krupe's wife was in charge, I did not trust anybody that worked in the town hall. I went in to help Amy make sandwiches for lunch and sagged with relief at the sight of Lola's car pulling into the driveway.

"I was really getting scared," I told her, "You've been gone so long."

"Sorry about that," she said, "But I was trying to make my trip look casual so I did some shopping along the way. Here, take this in, would you." She handed me a shopping bag and went back to the car for another sack.

"Those look good," Lola said, pointing to the sandwiches. She plopped her bag of groceries on the counter and sat down. Amy had cut the sandwiches into triangles and arranged them on a plate in the middle of the table. She had also cut up some watermelon and iced tea left beads of sweat on a pitcher.

"All this detecting has made me hungry," Lola said as she poured tea into a glass.

"What did you find out?" asked Amy, bouncing in her chair.

"Well, it's not exactly a typewriter, but an old Smith Corona word processor. It does have a ribbon, though, and it said SCM-50B on it."

"Wow, you were able to get the ribbon number? How did you do that?" I said.

"It was really easy, Maggie. I asked the girl for a copy of my land's legal description. Melinda Krupe came out of her office and asked me pointed questions, but when I told her I was thinking about replacing my garage and that I wanted to know exactly how close to the property line I could put a new one, she seemed satisfied. After all, she has seen my garage." Lola pointed out the window at the sagging building behind her house. This had been Allen's little kingdom and Lola could not bear to part with it, even though it was about to collapse under its own weight.

"Melinda would never figure out that I would never tear this down, it will fall down by itself first, so she believed my story. When the girl in the back had trouble finding the papers, Melinda went to help her. I just walked over and looked into the word processor while they were in the back. The ribbon is under a flap of plastic on the top. By the time they came out with my papers to make me a copy, I was sitting on a chair by the door."

"Good job, Lola!" I said. "Now, all I have to do is figure out how to get in and swap them, assuming I can get a new one, that is."

CHAPTER 36

▼

It was already Friday. I was running out of time. I wanted to head back to Spokane on Sunday—it was an all-day drive and I had told Rick I would be back at work Monday morning. I knew he wouldn't really mind if I needed a few more days off, but I was ready to go home. I yearned for my log house tucked into the foothills of Mt. Spokane. Soon it would be fall and the leaves would turn all kinds of vibrant colors. I wanted to stretch out in the hot tub on the deck in the back and look at the trees that surrounded my property. I wanted to sleep in my own bed and not be nervous every time I saw a policeman's car. I wanted to sit on the front porch and listen to my little creek, if it hadn't dried up completely by now, that is. Soon, soon, I told myself. Just get this problem solved.

After lunch I went to the library. I was pleased to see that they had a shelf of out-of-town phone directories. I took the one for Astoria, Oregon, and sat down to look up office supply stores.

My list of numbers in hand, I went to the pay phone at Jack's in Ocean Park again. I didn't want any record of my calls on Lola's phone. I found a store that carried the Smith Corona ribbon I needed with my first try. So far this project was easy.

I decided before heading to Astoria I would take a look around the town hall again. After all, I was a tourist. I would be expected to be doing some shopping.

I strolled along the main street. I went into a couple of little stores and bought a present for Sully. She was probably loving being able to lounge around in my house and watch TV with my animals, but she would expect special thanks, anyway. I found a great clock decorated with shells that I knew Rick would like. Burdened by bags, I stopped to catch my breath at a bench outside the town hall. I sat down and looked around.

The town hall was just one of the tenants in a long building that made up one city block in Ocean Side. Oliver Krupe's police station was on one side of the town hall, and a small coffee shop was on the other side, the last business in the block. I decided to go and in and have a cup.

"This is certainly an interesting building," I told the waitress.

"Yes, it's been here for years and years," she said.

"I love all the old lighting fixtures."

"I do too," she said, "But we've had a lot of trouble with the old wiring. We can't even have an alarm system or a space heater in here or all the breakers will trip."

I felt my antennae go up. No alarm system?

"The wiring has never been updated?"

"No, the landlord is too cheap. He's some rich Californian who bought this whole block as an investment and fixed it up with big ideas that went nowhere. He doesn't even live around here, so he doesn't care how much we suffer when it gets cold and damp."

"Well, you probably don't worry too much about getting broken into, what with the police station right there."

"No, we have never had a problem," the waitress said. "And it would be so easy to get in here. These windows go way up, somebody could push them open and just step in."

She pointed and I saw that the windows were of the simple double hung type—I could see the ropes that held the weights inside the frames. They were single panes, no storm windows or screens and I could see how they could be opened without much trouble. The bottom window was set low in the wall, too, fairly close to the boardwalk. The waitress was right; it looked like someone could just walk in through the window. Now I needed to go look at the town hall windows. If they were the same…maybe I could creep in tonight and switch out that ribbon.

"Thanks for the coffee; I enjoyed talking to you," I said.

"You're welcome," she said, "Enjoy your time in Ocean Side."

I walked back toward the Blazer, looking hard at the windows in the town hall as I passed. I could see that the wood had never been painted, that was good, the windows might not be stuck shut, but I also noted that there were locks in place. If I was going to try and get in I would need a window unlocked for me. Would Lola like to try and help me again?

CHAPTER 37

▼

Astoria was only a short drive across the Columbia River. The view from the bridge was awe-inspiring, but I hated to think what the trip might be like during a storm. The water was a long ways down. Within minutes of entering Astoria I was able to get the ribbon I needed and I headed back to Lola's with an plan in place.

"So, do you think you could go back and have Melinda notarize the copy she made you? Hopefully while she is doing that you could unlock a window for me. Then, later tonight I will try to sneak in and change the word processor ribbon."

"I can try, Maggie, but this is pretty frightening."

"I know. If it doesn't seem like you can do it without getting caught, don't take a chance. I can always come up with another plan." I had also picked up a glass cutter while in Astoria. Plan B would be to score the glass, then hopefully tap a piece out without shattering the whole thing and alerting the deputy I assumed would be on duty overnight in the police station. I had taken a class in stained glass art once and had learned how to cut glass. But, cutting a piece mounted in a frame that is upright would be tricky. I hoped Lola could open a lock for me.

"Well, I better go now, if I'm going to," she said. "Within an hour the office will be closed until Monday."

Once again Amy and I sat and waited. Lola was only gone a few minutes this time and she walked in with a smile on her face.

"That was perfect!" she said. "I got there at just the right time. Melinda was getting ready to close up for the night and had already sent the clerk home. She wasn't happy to see me with my request, but she couldn't refuse."

"So what happened, Lola?" Amy was leaning toward Lola, looking eager.

"Well, she was so intent on getting her stamp on my papers as quickly as she could that she didn't even notice me fiddling around with the windows. Then she practically pushed me out the door and locked it behind herself. She was ready to go home. I actually was able to unlock three of the windows, Maggie."

"Do you really think you will be able to get in there?" said Amy.

"I hope so, Amy. This will be one of our best chances to get some evidence of something happening to your parents other than that drowning story."

"But, aren't you worried about getting caught by a security system or something?"

"I'm hoping that the waitress that I talked to today was right and that there is no alarm. If there is, hopefully it will be an audible one that would provide me with enough warning that I could get out fast."

"Audible? What does that mean?" asked Lola.

"That means it's the kind of alarm that goes off with a loud noise. Some alarms are silent, they are only heard at the security company. Lola, do you know if there is any sort of company around here like that?"

"I'm not sure," she said, "But there could be something in Long Beach, that's for sure."

"How do you know so much about alarms, anyway?" asked Amy.

"I read lots of mystery and crime novels," I said. And, I thought, I have this incredible alarm system built into the house I bought. It is operated from a hidden apartment-like area in the basement the previous owner had put in when he and his wife built the house. It's a secure place I can get to from hidden stairways and passages that lead down from the house above. I haven't told anybody about it, though, not even Rick. It's just one of those secrets I really need to keep for now.

"I guess I'll just have to trust the waitress," I said.

"When are you going to do this?" asked Lola.

"I'm going to set my alarm for two a.m. Hopefully by then everybody will be asleep. I'm going to walk down, that will be quieter than driving. I'm glad that ribbon isn't very big. Now I better go see what kind of dark clothes I can put together."

CHAPTER 38

▼

After dinner I paced around Lola's kitchen. It was too early to go to bed but too late to get involved in a big project. Suddenly, I wanted chocolate chip cookies, like the ones my mother used to make when she was more concerned with making good food for her family than impressing other people. Lola was napping in her recliner; I would surprise her and Amy.

A short visit to her pantry found me all the supplies I needed. I turned her oven to preheat at 350 degrees and started to stir ingredients together.

The half cup of white sugar and half cup of packed light brown sugar went into a bowl. I added half a cup of Crisco and stirred. Next I mixed in an egg and a half a teaspoon of REAL VANILLA EXTRACT (I could hear my mother's voice saying how she hated the imitation stuff) and a couple of tablespoons of brewed coffee. If there hadn't been any coffee I just would have thrown in a couple of tablespoons of water. I mixed a half a teaspoon of baking soda and a half of teaspoon of salt into a generous cup of flour, about a cup and an eighth, and stirred that into the sugar mixture. I poured a small bag of chocolate chips in next. The recipe called for half of a cup of chopped walnuts, too, but Lola did not have any. That was just as well, I didn't know if Amy had a nut allergy. Besides, the cookies would taste fine without the nuts.

I took a teaspoon out of Lola's silverware drawer and used it to drop blobs of dough onto cookie sheets. My mother baked them at 350 degrees for 10 minutes, but that made a crispy, brown, cookie. I liked mine softer, so generally baked them for about eight minutes.* I just put a few in for the first baking; I wasn't sure how accurate the settings on Lola's oven were.

"What is that lovely smell?" asked Lola, walking into the kitchen and rubbing her eyes. "I guess I fell asleep in my chair."

"I hope it's okay," I said, lifting baked cookies off the baking sheet and putting them on a rack to cool. "I was so hungry for chocolate chip cookies that I raided your pantry and made some."

Lola nodded and opened her mouth to reply when Amy walked into the kitchen, head held high and sniffing the air like a retriever who just caught the scent of a downed duck.

"That is perfectly all right," Lola said. "Let me make some fresh coffee and we'll gorge."

When I finally went to bed I didn't expect to be able to get any sleep what with the chocolate and the coffee, but I must have drifted off right away, as the alarm startled me awake. It took me a few minutes to get my bearings and remember what I was going to do. I slipped out of bed and got dressed.

I didn't have any black slacks with me, but a pair of dark brown ones would do. I had a hooded black sweatshirt with sleeves long enough to pull down over my hands. Only my face and my feet in their Birkenstocks would be exposed.

After six trips to the bathroom, piddling only nerves on the last five stops, I was out the door.

There was a ghost of a breeze blowing, stirring the bushes and trees. I was glad for the little bit of noise that helped cover the noise my feet made. There was a partial moon giving skimpy light and the clouds blew across it, occasionally turning the dark night even darker.

I walked along the side of the road trying to hurry without running. There were no cars to be seen, or any other people, either, but if I were to be seen I didn't want to attract any undue attention.

It wasn't far to the main street of Ocean Side and the town hall was dark. I fingered the typewriter ribbon in my pocket and hoped I would able to change it without any light. It had not occurred to me to bring a flashlight and I cursed my lapse.

There were lights on in the sheriff's office and I could see somebody sitting in a chair. But, he had his feet on the desk and his eyes were shut. Praying that he was asleep, I stepped onto the boardwalk.

The boards complained softly underfoot and I held my breath. There was no way for me to keep an eye on the deputy and break into the town hall at the same time. I hoped luck would be on my side.

It was easy for me to tell from the outside which of the three windows that Lola had unlocked; at times it was nice to be tall. Two were on the right side of the door and one on the left. I crossed my fingers and went to the left window first. I wasn't quite sure how to do this, there was nothing to grab hold of; these windows were not meant to be opened from the outside. I stared at them for a minute. The bottom sash on the top half of the window was in front of the top sash of the lower pane, so it was impossible to push the window up that way. There was no way to get my fingers underneath the bottom sash on the lower pane either, it was settled into the sill. I hadn't thought about bringing any sort of pry bar either. What a useless burglar I was. Oh, to have Henry's claws about now!

I stood and thought. Maybe if I put my palms against the glass and pushed up. I spit on my hands a bit and rubbed them together. I laid both palms against the glass and tried to concentrate on pushing up, not in. No good. The window creaked alarmingly, but it did not budge. Okay. There were two more to try. I moved across the door to the window on the right. Again, push up, not in, I lectured myself. This window slid up about three inches and stopped. Rats, it would not go up any further. I squatted down to try again when I heard footsteps.

Crabwise, I scuttled along the boardwalk and across the front of the now-silent coffee shop to the end of the walkway. I dropped to the ground and sat with my legs crossed, hiding my white feet, I hoped. I heard a door open and the footsteps grew louder, and closer. Every cell in my body yelled, "RUN!" Instead, I tucked my head down, pulled my sweatshirt hood up and over my face and tried to breathe silently. The moon slid behind the clouds and the darkness thickened.

The footsteps came closer and stopped. I could smell cigarette smoke. I let the hood of the sweatshirt slide down a fraction of an inch. The moon was peeking out of the clouds again and I could just discern the outline of a man in the whisper of moonlight. I caught a dull metallic glint at his waist area. That must be the deputy and I was seeing his sidearm. I could hear him inhaling and I could see the glow from the cigarette's tip momentarily brighten.

How long does a cigarette burn, anyway? I swore the sun would be up before this guy finished. I finally heard a little flicking noise and out of the corner of my eye saw a cigarette butt bounce around in the dirt, creating a little shower of sparks before it went out. The footstep sounds started again, this time moving away from me. I heard a door open and close, then all was still. Moving in tiny increments, I allowed my head to come up and all the way out of my sweatshirt.

There was nobody standing on the boardwalk where the deputy had been enjoying his break.

I got to my feet and crept back onto the boardwalk. I realized the window in the town hall was still open those three inches. A shiver ran down my back. The deputy must not have seen it; I peeked in the sheriff's office window and he was back in his chair with his eyes closed and feet up, a girly magazine in his hand. His other hand was moving around under the magazine; I did not want to know why. I could imagine what was going on though and smiled. Hopefully he would be distracted enough not to hear any noise I made.

There was only one more window I could try. I pushed the second window closed and went to the third one Lola had unlocked for me. My mouth was dry as cotton. I had to stand for a minute and think about lemon meringue pie before I could conjure up enough spit to dampen my hands.

Again I crouched down and laid my palms on the glass. "Come on, baby, do it this time," I whispered to myself. The window moved up about six inches, and stopped. I pushed again and it crept up another inch. My hands were dry again. I fingered the glass cutter in my pocket and wondered, did I dare do that? One more time, one more push, then I would have to go for the cutter. But, now that the bottom sash was up out of the sill I could get my fingers under it. That would be easier than trying to move the window by pushing up on the glass.

I slipped my fingers under the sash and lifted. I had to fight to stop the scream. There was something sharp that ran across the width of the window, nearly cutting my fingers, must be a moisture seal of some type. I went back to the second window and pushed it open again, but it had the same type of strip running across the bottom. I pushed it shut. I would have to go back to my first method.

I took a moment to breathe. My legs were quivering and my arms ached. I wanted to sit down and weep, but I had come this far, so I would try one more time. I went back to the last window I had tried. It had opened the most, I hoped it was my best bet.

I could see a clock on a desk inside the town hall. Its red digital numbers said two-thirty. I could not believe that it had only been thirty minutes since I crawled out of bed at Lola's. I felt like I had been on this boardwalk for hours.

Maybe if I stood and tried to pull up on the glass, maybe that would work. Taking a deep breath, I wet my hands again and placed them on the window and pulled up. The window groaned and I echoed it inside my head. "Don't hear that," I instructed the deputy in a whisper, "That was just the building settling."

The window made noise, but it moved, just another inch or so. I stopped and considered. It was open about eight inches, but that still looked too small for me to crawl through. I had to get it open some more. I pulled up on the glass again and the window moved up a fraction of an inch and stopped. I let my breath out in a sigh. This was not going to work. One more time, just one more, then I would go around to the back of the building and look for a back window that I might be able to cut the glass out of.

This time I put just the tips of my fingers on the edge of the bottom sash and lifted. I hardly had enough leverage on the edge of the sash and did not think this was going to work either. I tried to lift up with just a little more force. For a heartbeat the window did not move, then suddenly it gave and slid up until it was almost half way open. That was more than far enough; I could get in.

One body part at a time, first a leg, then and an arm and finally my head. Now for the really scary part. If this building had a security system, the opening of the window might have triggered it, or there might be motion sensors inside. Once I was in the building I would be trapped. I teetered on the sill for a few seconds. The night remained still. I let the rest of my body slide into the building.

I was all the way inside, sitting on the floor hunched against the wall. The wind had tossed the clouds aside and now there was just enough moonlight sliding in through the windows to allow me to see the word processor sitting against the side wall of the office.

There had been no audible alarm, and even if I had triggered a silent one I would still have a few seconds to change the ribbon. I stood up and took three long steps across the office to the word processor.

Like Lola had said, there was just a flap covering the place where the ribbon went. I lifted it up. It took some fiddling, but finally the used ribbon came out. I put it in my pocket with the glass cutter and pulled out the new one. I put it in, and pushed. My fingers were quivering from the force I had used to open the window and were not working well. The ribbon did not snap into place. I pushed on it again, but it remained out of place. What was the key to this? Again I cursed my lack of a flashlight. I might have been able to cover the lens with my hand and let just a trickle of light out so I could see what I was doing.

Every second the risk increased. At any time that deputy might decide he needed another cigarette. This ribbon just has to go in. I wiggled it around, took it out and put it back, and pushed down again. No luck. This was stupid, to come this far and not be able to get this ribbon in. "Stupid thing," I muttered, and smacked it with my hand.

Snick. The ribbon popped into place. The room spun and I waited a moment for the lightheaded rush of relief to subside. I closed the cover over the ribbon, marveling. I had done it. Now to get out of here without getting caught.

I flowed out the window onto the boardwalk like a stream of water. The window slid down much more easily than it had opened. Within seconds I was headed back across the street toward Lola's. Sweat was running down my back and I was breathing hard.

I heard a door slam and a voice yelling, "Hey, you! What are you doing? Get out of there."

I froze. It was the deputy; had he seen me? I didn't move. If he was shouting at me I would soon know about it. I heard some crashing and banging behind me. The deputy continued to yell, but his voice was fading. I slowly turned around, then eased over behind a scraggly bush. It wasn't much cover, but I hoped it would shield me from view.

The deputy came around from behind the building. "Damned masked bugger, anyway," I heard him say. He went back inside his office. I waited for a few minutes to make sure he wasn't coming back out, then stepped out of the bushes. A hint of movement caught my eye and I saw what he had been yelling at. A large raccoon, not bothered by the human voice, went bumbling across the road, headed for somebody else's garbage can to raid.

Thoroughly unnerved by now, I ran the rest of the way to Lola's house. My bed there had never looked or felt so good. I looked at the clock again, two-forty-five. I peeled off my sweat-soaked clothes and dropped into bed. Whew, what a night.

CHAPTER 39

▼

Saturday morning and I was almost out of time. Something would have to happen today if I was going to be able to give Amy any help.

We sat at the table and unrolled the typewriter ribbon. Marty had been right; this was a single-use ribbon. We could read it sort of like a stock market ticker tape, all the words and numbers running along the tape from left to right. It was slow going, but finally, close to the middle of the ribbon, we saw the names Bethel and George Armstrong, along with their dates of death and the reported details of them being drowned.

"This proves it, doesn't it?" said Amy. "Now we know my parents aren't dead. Let's go get that Oliver Krupe." She jumped up and headed for the door.

"Wait, Amy," I said, "We can't do that. This is just proof than somebody fabricated their death certificates; it doesn't prove anything else."

"Then why else would the sheriff's wife be typing up fake death certificates; that's not her job. I want to know what happened to my mom and dad." Amy's face crumpled and she burst into tears.

I looked at Lola. We needed more help than just us. I went to the phone.

I had no idea if I could get hold of anybody at the closest FBI office, which was in Seattle. I was not surprised to get a recording, telling me to push various numbers for various services. I let the message run, there really was no choice that fit our problem and no option to push 0 or some other number to get a human being. But, I remembered what an telephone operator I had me once when I needed to talk to a service representative at Qwest. "Just listen to the message twice," she told me. "After the second, or sometimes the third repetition of the message, your call will be answered by a person. The system has to be set up to take calls from those people who still have rotary phones and are unable to push a button as instructed."

I had tried it and it had worked. The Qwest service rep had been a bit non-plussed to have a person on the other end and I did not share with her how I had gotten through to her. Today I would try the tactic with the FBI's answering message. I sat and listened to their recording.

Finally a voice said, "FBI, Seattle office," "How can I direct your call?"

The trick had worked. Giving Amy and Lola a thumbs-up, I told the operator that I had a suspicious disappearance of two people and some signs that might indicate a dishonest cop. She said, "Thank you," and I listened to elevator music for a few minutes.

"Special Agent Randolph," said a brisk-sounding voice.

"Hello," I said, "My name is Maggie Jackson and I'm calling from Ocean Side."

"Yes? How can I help you?"

I spent the next ten minutes telling Agent Randolph the whole story. "So, I was able to get hold of the ribbon from the word processor they used to make what we think are the false death certificates. But, our problem is that there is nobody we can turn to for help, as the sheriff's wife works in the town hall and she probably did the typing. We think the sheriff is involved in this couple's disappearance because he refuses to help find them; he won't even let the peoples' daughter file a missing person report."

There was a moment of silence on the phone. "That does sound a little funny," SA Randolph said.

"Can you come down here and do some checking for us?"

"I'll see what I can do. It will take me awhile to drive down, but I could be there by this afternoon. I need to talk to my supervisor and see what he wants me to do. I'll call you back and let you know."

"Do you want this number?" I asked.

SA Randolph laughed. "That's okay," he said, "I have it."

Yeah, I bet you do, I thought, as I replaced the receiver. "Well, we may be see-ing the FBI later today. That was a Special Agent Randolph. He said he will try and come down."

"Finally we will get some answers," said Amy.

"I hope so. In the meantime, I'm going to take Henry out for a walk. I'll be back in a few minutes."

CHAPTER 40

▼

It was another lovely day on the ocean. The tide was on the way in and it seemed each wave reached higher up the beach. We talked along and watched the water and the sea birds. There were lots of people out on the sand today too, kids dashing in and out of the chilly water, the adults keeping a close eye on them, and a dog or too dashing about.

One dog dug like crazy up in the dunes and it took his owner several attempts before he was able to drag him away. Henry was not really afraid of this dog, but there was a narrow band of fur standing up along his back as he watched him.

We strolled for almost an hour. It was so peaceful out here; I could almost forget all the ugliness of the last days. But, it had not been a totally awful trip. It was nice to be able to spend so much time with Lola. It would have been nice to have the same relationship with my mother, but I feared that was not to be. My sister, Beth, had run away to Ireland to escape my mother, and I just tried to stay out of her way. After all, I get tired of being criticized for every move I make. Mom had even been upset that I was leaving Phil after the assault and his crimes were uncovered. I could still hear her voice telling me I didn't want to have a divorce "on my record," did I? I was glad when she moved out of Spokane and back to San Diego, where she had grown up. To her, San Diego was the only city that had the "right" sort of people living in it.

The west coast was wonderful; I loved being able to get out onto the beach and smell the salt air. But, I was also feeling the tug of home. Rick waited for me there and he might be the answer to a new life.

Henry's shoulder had healed well. There was still no fur on the spot, but the bullet furrow was clean and dry. His limp was gone, too.

I stood and watched the sky blue that melted into the deeper blue/green of the ocean. I suddenly envisioned a quilt made from wavy pieces of fabric, light blue at the top and fading into darker blue at the bottom. Then maybe appliqué some dolphins on it? Beth would love that. She has a thing for dolphins.

Cheered at the idea for a new quilt and feeling like there was progress being made at last for Amy, I headed back to Lola's.

CHAPTER 41

▼

I felt calm as I walked up Lola's driveway. With any luck the FBI was on the way. They should be able to get some answers from Oliver Krupe and start the process in motion to find the Armstrongs.

"Lola, Amy, I'm back." The house was silent. That was funny, they had to be here. Lola's car was still in the driveway. Maybe they had gone for a walk, too.

I unclipped Henry from his harness; walks always made him hungry, he would head for his food bowl in the kitchen.

I went into my room and stopped short. This time everything was upside down. Even the sewing boxes had been emptied and overturned. But, once again the searchers had been frustrated in their search. I had moved the papers they sought; a quick feel behind the headboard told me they were still taped in place where I had put them. "Ha!" I said, "Foiled you again!"

I could hear Henry talking in the kitchen. It sounded like he was looking out the window at somebody he knew. He loved that game, he would meow and bob his head. If the person said, "Hi, Henry," he would bleat and bob again. Whoever it was really knew how to play the game, he meowed over and over again.

"Who is it, Henry?" I asked him on my way to the kitchen.

Once again I stopped short, then fell to my knees. Lola was lying on the floor, her breathing labored and a pool of blood widening under her head. I could see a piece of paper stuffed down the front of her shirt.

"Lola, oh, my God, are you okay?" She did not respond and I could see now that she was unconscious. And where was Amy? What had happened here? I jumped up and ran for the phone, but then I stopped. Oliver Krupe would be no help, what was I going to do. Dr. Grant's name was written on the outside of the phone book's front cover. I crossed my fingers and dialed. Thank God, Dr. Grant answered.

"Lola's lying on the floor, unconscious. Can you come over, please?"

He didn't waste any time asking questions, but said, "I'll be right there, Maggie. You call the police."

I hung up without answering and went back to Lola. She was moving around some and moaning softly.

"Don't move, Lola," I said, dropping back down onto the floor next to her. "I called Dr. Grant. He'll be right over."

Lola turned her head and I could see where the blood had come from. There was a nasty-looking lump just behind one ear with a cut in the center of it. The bleeding had slowed to an ooze, though, I was glad to see.

"Amy," Lola said, "They got Amy."

"Who, who got her? What do you mean?"

"It was Carl, he took her."

She moved again and I heard a crackling noise. The piece of paper in her shirt; I had forgotten about it. I pulled it out.

> "If you want to see your little friend Amy again you will leave town and take her with you. Don't talk about the Armstrongs again, either. Do this and we may let Amy and Lola live. Have your decision ready when we call you later."

The note was not signed. I heard the crunch of tires in the driveway. I ran to the door and let Dr. Grant in. I took him to Lola and heard his soothing voice talking to her. I sat in the living room and waited, wringing my hands and feeling desperate.

"Well, she should go to the hospital, but she refuses," he said, walking into the living room. She says that Amy will not be safe unless she stays home. I don't know what's going on here, Maggie, but I am worried about both you and Lola."

"It's a mess, Dr. Grant. I don't dare call the police about this, because I think that Oliver Krupe is involved. But, I did call the FBI this morning and there is an agent coming here, I hope. Do you think it would be okay for me to leave Lola for a little while? There is somebody else I can talk to, but I don't want to do it on the phone." I handed him the note to read. "As you can see, I need to be careful."

Dr. Grant frowned. "Lola took a pretty good smack on the head, but she's a hard-headed lady. Tell you what. I can forward my calls here for awhile and as long as there are no more emergencies, I can stay with Lola. He picked up the phone, but before he could pick it up it ran under his hand. "Hello? Yes, just a minute."

"It's an agent Randolph for you," he said, handing me the receiver.

"Maggie Jackson? This is Special Agent Randolph, we spoke earlier? I talked to my supervisor and he said he doesn't think you problem is one we can help you with, so…"

I cut him off. "My friend has been kidnapped, you can help with that, right?"

"What?" Agent Randolph's tone had sharpened. "Who has been kidnapped and are you sure?"

I read him the note. "Now can you come help us?"

"Yes, I am sure I can," he said. "I'll talk to my supervisor again, but I am sure I will see you this afternoon. Good-bye."

I handed the phone to Dr. Owens. "The FBI will be here later," I said, as Owen dialed the phone and spoke a few words into it.

"There," he said, "My calls are now routed to come in here. I need you to call every half hour or so and if I'm not here you will need to come back. Lola needs to be awakened every two hours if she goes to sleep to make sure there is no ongoing brain injury, but you know about that, anyway."

"Thanks so much, Dr. Grant, you may be saving all our lives. Don't let that cat bug you too much." Henry had draped himself over Dr. Grant's shoulders and he was absentmindedly petting him.

"When the FBI guy gets here, tell him everything you can. Tell him I went to Glen Gunnison, the deputy, to try and get some help finding Amy. Meanwhile, I'll check in with you at least every half hour." I patted my pocket to make sure my cell phone was there.

I ran out the door and got in the Blazer.

CHAPTER 42

▼

Deputy Glen Gunnison was my only hope here in Ocean Side. I tucked the ransom note, which was what I had to call it, into my pocket and drove to his house.

But, the house was silent, there was nobody home. Hoping he was on duty, I headed for the sheriff's office.

Once there I could see Glen Gunnison was inside. But, Oliver Krupe was also there. He did not appear to be on duty; he was not wearing his uniform. Now what was I going to do?

Just wait, I guess. I sat across the street and watched, nearly sweating blood with impatience. Until Oliver left the office I would have no chance to talk to Glen. But for the moment I would just have to wait. I'll give them five minutes, I decided, then I'll have to do something to get Glen out where I can talk to him.

The seconds crawled. I knew that Dr. Grant would tell SA Randolph what was going on, but I was afraid Amy would run out of time before he got here.

A red GEO Metro crossed my line of sight. It was Carl Rolley. He parked in front of the office where it said, "No Parking" and went in.

Great. Now they were both in there. But, within moments Carl and Oliver came out, got into the GEO and left. Now was my chance. I got out of the Blazer and started across the street, as fast as I could go.

A fat woman carrying a whimpering child was quicker though, and she beat me in the door. I dropped into a chair by the door. Again I had to wait for what seemed like an eternity while Glen tried to explain to her that he could not arrest a child for throwing sand at her child, that was how kids were on the beach. He told her to take her child to play someplace away from the other child. He was sorry, but that's all he could do. She stomped out, muttering about worthless policemen. If only you knew, I thought.

Glen started to make a note then looked up when I jumped to my feet. "Maggie. What can I do for you?"

I pulled the paper I had found stuffed in Lola's shirt out of my pocket and handed it to him. "Read this. I think Oliver and Carl Rolley kidnapped Amy Sanders and attacked my aunt. I found her lying in a pool of blood with this stuffed down the front of her clothes and she told me Carl did it."

I watched his face while he read. His expression went from surprise to shock to anger. "Who wrote this? What in the hell is going on, anyway?"

"Whoever took Amy and attacked my aunt, that's who. My room was searched, again, but they did not find what they wanted. I'm assuming they were looking for the papers I was able to find at the town hall; the ones that cost Clarice Miller her life. And who are those people? Carl Rolley and Oliver Krupe, that's who." I was standing in front of Glen's desk, leaning against the top and yelling into his face. "Your boss is crooked. He just left here with Carl Rolley. Where are they going? Did they say?"

Glen stared at me. "Ollie said that he and Carl had a fish they needed to gut. But, no, he didn't say exactly where he was going, either."

"Does Krupe even go fishing? I can't imagine he would get his hands that dirty."

"No, and I wondered about that. But, you never know with Ollie. Still, that doesn't mean he's involved in this," Glen said, pointing to the ransom note.

"What? How can you say that?" I said. "He has been nothing but obstructive since the moment Amy showed up wondering where her parents are. If he isn't involved in their disappearance, what is he doing? Why is he refusing to help her?"

Glen shook his head. "I don't know," he said. "I tried to look into things for Amy, but when I saw the death certificates..."

"Which were FALSE, for crying out loud," I hollered. "I got the word processor ribbon out of the town hall office and the evidence was right there. Those certificates were typed in that office, not at the county seat where it should have been done. There were also things that indicated that Melinda Krupe helped Carl Rolley get hold of all the Armstrong's possessions, from cars and a truck to their trailer and their land. You have to help me find Amy and stop Oliver and Carl."

I flopped down into the chair, tears threatening. One woman was dead, my aunt was injured, another young woman was kidnapped and I felt like it was all my fault. Amy probably would have eventually given up and gone home, if I hadn't butted in. She had asked me to help, that was true, but I could have been smart, I could have said no. I have to start jumping away from trouble, I thought.

"The typewriter ribbon? What are you talking about?" said Glen.

"Oh, that's not important right now. I don't have time to tell you the whole story, but I was able to see where those death certificates had been hand typed and not run off a computer printer like they should have been. They are fake, probably to allow Carl and Oliver to be able to steal and sell Amy's parents' property."

Glen was shaking his head and frowning.

I stood up. "That's enough about that. I have to go and look for Amy," I said. "I don't know where I am going to start, but I can't just sit here while you try to make up your mind what to believe."

I walked out of the sheriff's office and got in the Blazer. I pulled my cell phone out of my pocket and called Lola's house. She was doing okay and Dr. Grant was still there. I told him I would check back in another half an hour. I turned the key, but before the engine started the passenger door opened and Glen Gunnison got in.

"I called the night guy to come in early. I told him I had a personal emergency, which is almost true. I think the first place to start looking for Amy would be at Ollie's place. That garage of his is like a fortress."

I felt a surge of relief. Nothing like having an armed escort when you go on a rescue mission.

Glen and I were quiet on the way to Oliver Krupe's house. I had said my piece more than once and I could tell that he was still chewing it around.

"Stop and park over there," said Glen, when we were about a block from Oliver's house. "Let's walk the rest of the way. It will be harder for him to see us, if he's there."

Glen led me down an alley that ran across the street from where Oliver and his wife lived. We walked past the driveway leading to their garage, then Glen pulled me behind a thick rhododendron bush.

"We can go around this way," he said, pointing at a narrow opening in the bushes. "This will take us up to the side of the garage without our having to actually walk down Oliver's alley."

Oliver's house looked empty, its windows dark and no cars parked in the driveway. The garage squatted in back, its doors firmly chained and padlocked shut. We came out of the bushes at the back corner.

"Last time I was here Oliver was complaining about a crack in the wall," Glen whispered. "I was standing with my back to the front door and I could see a spot somewhere back in this area where light was coming in. If Oliver hasn't patched it, we might be able to see in. He usually leaves the light on inside, too, that'll help."

We started going over the back wall of the garage. I saw many a spider and beetle, but no crack. I was pulling myself up to my feet when a flash of light caught my eye.

"Glen, over here," I hissed. "I think I found something."

Glen came over and put his eye to the place where I had seen the light. "Yes, this is it. I can see inside."

"Is Amy in there; is anybody in there?" Glen shook his head and stepped away from the garage. I hunkered down and looked in. The garage was silent. I squatted there peeking through the crack until my knees screamed for mercy. There was no motion of any kind in the garage that I could see, either.

"I don't think there is anybody in there. Where else can we look?"

Glen said, "I know that Carl has a place on the bay side of the peninsula. It's not really a house, just sort of a hunting shack, but it would be a good place to hide out. Let's take your car back to your aunt's. You can check on her and then we can take my car. I don't think Carl has ever seen it and your Blazer sticks out like a sore thumb, being new in the area and all."

That made good sense to me and I wanted to check on Lola, anyway.

"Lola is doing okay," said Owen Grant, holding the door open for me. "She slept for a little while, but she's awake now. I did give her something for pain, though, so if she seems a bit drunk don't be concerned."

Lola did look a little tipsy, her smile goofy. "How do you feel?"

"Better now," she said. "Owen gave me a lil' shot." She giggled.

"That's good." Lola was more than a little drunk. We would be able to laugh at this later, I hoped. Her eyes started to close. She would probably sleep some more. "I'm going back out to look for Amy. I will let Owen know if I find anything and he can tell you."

"'S dangerous," she said, her speech slurred.

"I'll be okay. I'm going with Deputy Gunnison."

Her eyes flew open, then closed again. "Glen…don't…'s dangerous," she said again, then started to snore softly.

I went to my room and pulled all my notes and information off the back of the headboard. I used Lola's fax machine to make a copy of the ransom note and all the other papers I had gathered. I tried to hold the note by the edges only, but feared any fingerprints that might have been on the paper were gone by now.

Still, it didn't hurt to be careful. I put my original copies back in their hiding place and went back to the kitchen where Owen Grant sat reading the paper.

"She's asleep, Owen. I'm going with Deputy Gunnison to look for Amy. When the FBI guy gets here give him all this stuff." I handed him the packet. "I have my cell phone and I'll keep checking with you. In the note that was left with Lola, they said they were going to call here, but I doubt that will happen. If they do, though, you can tell them that I am thinking about leaving like they said to do, that I'm walking on the beach to think, whatever you think will work. I'll leave that up to you. Are you still planning on hanging around here?"

"Yes. I'll stay for another couple of hours, if I can. I think Lola is going to be fine, but I just want to be sure. It's actually kind of peaceful here. This is the first chance I have had in weeks to read the paper all the way through. Are you expecting somebody from the FBI to actually come down here?"

"I'm pretty sure we'll see somebody. I talked to a Special Agent Randolph this morning and he said if his supervisor thought it appropriate, he was going to come down. Especially now with Amy missing, kidnapped, I should say, I would bet he'll be down. I have to go; I'll talk to you later. Call me if you need to." I wrote down the number for him. "Thanks." I ran out the door.

Glen was leaning against his car, waiting for me. I climbed into the passenger seat and was relieved to see the clear plastic partition separating the front seats from the back ones. If we caught a bad guy we'd have a place to put him.

"You don't think Carl will recognize this car? It just shouts COP to me."

"He might, but it won't matter. He thinks that I just do what Ollie tells me to do and Carl has nothing to fear from Ollie."

As Glen backed out of Lola's driveway I looked up at the sky. Clouds were starting to mass on the horizon and the ocean was strangely calm. I looked past her house to the ocean where tiny waves broke on the sand.

"Looks like we may be in for a storm," I said. "I hope we find Amy before it breaks." Storms that came in from the ocean could be ferocious. The wind would howl at near-hurricane strength and the now-placid sea would start to churn. Soon the waves would be cresting at foot measurements, rather than inches. The bigger they got and the harder the wind blew, especially if the tide was coming in at the time, the farther up the beach they would come. Lola had actually had water over her lawn a time or two and she lived well back of the tules, which were sort the boundary for the usual high tide point. Huge driftwood logs sat along the edges of the tules, evidence of the power of wind and water. The rain would fall in torrents, too. If Amy were being held outdoors it could get very chilly for her and she could be at risk for hypothermia. I hoped Glen had a good idea where she might be and that we could find her.

Glen turned off the street in front of Lola's toward the Willapa Bay side of the North Beach Peninsula. "Carl's place is not right on the water, but on the other side of the road that runs along the bay," Glen said. "It's sort of buried in the woods; it would be a perfect hiding place."

It didn't take long before Glen said, "Here it is," and pulled into a driveway that was really just a couple of ruts, with grass growing up in the middle. The clouds had now covered the sky and the wind was picking up. The forest looked dark and forbidding.

The woods around Spokane are mostly pine and fir. There could be places where the undergrowth was thick and hard to get through, but nothing like here, where things grew and grew and stayed green all year around. These woods looked primeval to me. Thick cedar bushes and leafy bushes hung with vines swept the sides of the car as we moved into the along the rutted driveway. Moss hung from branches and there was a wet-blanket smell to the air. If a dinosaur had stepped out in front of us I would not have been surprised.

We came around a bend and I got my first glimpse of Carl's "place." Glen had been right, there certainly was no real house here. Rather it was a series of shacks, some small and tumble-down, some larger and in better repair. Carl would probably never bother to tear anything down, just built something new and let the other one rot into the ground. It looked like he lived in an old travel trailer that was perched on concrete blocks at what must have been the rear of his property, as the trees and bushes grew right up to the back side of the trailer. Vines grew around the wheels and axles, appearing to tie them to the ground. There was a faint light coming from one tiny window and through a small window in the door.

Glen stopped the car before we were all the way into the clearing in front of the trailer. He pulled it off into the bushes where it would be out of sight. "Look," he said, "Beside the trailer. That looks like Ollie's prowl car."

"It does. Well. I'm not in the least bit surprised. I was pretty sure he was in cahoots with Carl and this pretty much decides it for me. What do we do now?"

"Let's see if we can check out the buildings before we try and confront Carl and Ollie," said Glen. "Let's start over here," he pointed to his left, "and circle around to the trailer."

"Don't we need some help here?" I asked. "Can you call for back-up?"

"Not really. The only other deputy is at the station and he will need to stay there if case there's another call. Let's see if we can figure out what's going on first, then I'll call him if I need to."

The wind had picked up in speed. The tops of the trees twisted madly above us, but they grew so thickly that there was no breeze blowing around us when we got out of the car. Glen eased the doors shut and whispered to me, "You start with the first building here and I'll start from the other end and work back toward you. Take this." He handed me a pen-size flashlight, like the ones I used to use to check pupil reactions in my intensive care unit hospital patients. "Stay where you are and flash this toward me if you find anything. I'll come to you."

I could hear rain starting to spatter on the leaves above me. It would be awhile, though, before any water made it to the ground. I shouldn't get too wet.

The first building was roofless and most of the floor had rotted away. There was nothing there but a couple of huge banana slugs, well-named for both their color and size, leaving slime trails on the splintered wood. I moved on to the next spot. This building, too, was not much more than sagging walls held up by the branches of a tree that was growing up through what was left of the floor.

The next shack looked more promising. The glass was gone from the windows, but they had been covered with criss-crossed boards. I was able to see in, though, and there was enough light filtering in to give me a pretty good look at the interior. It actually had a roof and floor, but it was empty. I stepped away and looked over to where Glen had started searching. He was standing by what looked almost like a real garage, waving his arms at me. He walked over to me and pulled me behind the building I had just been looking into.

"I found her," he hissed. "She's tied to a chair in the garage over there."

"Oh, my, God, that's wonderful," I said. "What do we do now? Call for help?"

"Yes," he said, "I'll need some help."

Had night come? Why was I suddenly seeing stars overhead? And, if those were stars, why were they red and purple and green?

CHAPTER 43

▼

Oh, boy. Now I had an idea how Lola was feeling. But what happened? One minute I was talking to Glen, the next minute I'm…where? I opened my eyes and the world spun around me. I closed them again. With a shaky hand I reached up and touched my head behind my left ear. There was quite a goose egg there, but the skin felt intact, though a bit spongy. I lay still and tried to think. It felt like a wood floor under my cheek and the air had a dusty, dry smell. Rain pattered on a roof overhead, so I must be inside somewhere. Then I thought about Glen. Where was he? Had somebody clobbered him over the head, too? Maybe he was nearby.

I opened my left eye and the spinning was gone. I risked the right eye. Okay, good. No more spinning. The pain, which had been overwhelming, subsided somewhat into a ferocious throbbing. I rolled over onto my side and put my hand flat on the floor. I pushed myself to a sitting position, then froze, closing my eyes until the wave of nausea faded. I opened my eyes again and looked around. I was alone.

It looked like I was in the building I had last looked in and it was completely empty. I could see the crossed boards over the window holes. There were scrape marks in the dust on the floor, and from the looks of my clothes, I had been drug in here and dumped. My cell phone was still in my pocket, but I couldn't get a signal. Whoever hit me must have known that, or it would be gone. Well, so what. Now I would just leave and go look for Glen. Then we would need to get to the car and call for help.

My legs quivered when I stood up and I had to fight off another bout of nausea, but I could walk. I went over to the door. Locked. Gee, what a surprise. I looked around. The openings around the boards over the windows were too small to squeeze through; I was trapped.

I sank back down on the floor and allowed myself a moment of self-pity. "Dumb ass," I muttered, "You should have waited for the FBI guy. Now you got both yourself and Glen Gunnison in trouble." I wept a few bitter tears, then dried my eyes on my sleeve. "Enough of that, now figure out how to get out of here and get some help."

The door was sturdy, it didn't even move when I pushed against it. I tried kicking it, but all that did was make my foot sore and made my head pound sickeningly. I would have to see if I could get out a window.

The bottom of the lowest window was about mid chest high and about two feet by two feet square. If I could get the boards off I would be able to get out that way. I looked at them, squinting hard in the meager light.

The boards had been fastened to the window frames on the inside. This made me think that the place had been prepared in advance as a prison, but that might actually work to my advantage. There was nothing to stand on and there was no way I could apply any push to the boards, but maybe I could pull on off. I reached up and tried one, but the board did not move, it was securely fastened in place.

I stood for a minute and pondered. There was nothing at all in the building that I could use for a lever. I went back to look at the boards again. They had been screwed in place and the screws looked new. They would come out fairly easily, no corrosion yet, but I still would need a screwdriver.

While I stood and stared at the windows, I stuck my hands in my pockets, hitting my car keys. I pulled them out and grinned. I must have just automatically stuck them in my pocket when we had gone back to Lola's to get Glen's car. I had gotten in the habit of not putting my keys in my purse when I got out of the car. I had my purse grabbed out of a shopping basket one time years ago and I was still grateful that the thief had not also gotten my keys. That would have given them entry into my house, the veterinary clinic, my friend Georgia's house, what an additional nightmare that had been. But, now that habit had worked in my favor. I had my keys with me. I might just get out of this place yet.

My dad had died young, and my mother, in a fit of despondent grief, had pretty much immediately gotten rid of everything that had been his. I had ended up with just a pocket watch as a remembrance. But, when I first started to drive, he had given me an odd little tool to carry on my key chain. It was a flat disk a little smaller in diameter than a silver dollar. It had the word Cole on one side and on the other side had a four-leaf clover. Around the edge on the clover side it said: POCKET SCREWDRIVER FITS MOST SCREWS. There were four tabs coming out of the edge of the disk at the twelve, three, six and nine o'clock positions. Each one was a different width to fit a different screw. I had never thought it would really be good for anything, but carried it because he gave it to me and because of the four-leaf clover. Now I could use some of that luck.

The screws in the boards were standard head, I was relieved to see. This little tool would be no good with a Phillips screw. The biggest tab looked like it would be the best one to try. I set to work.

The screws backed out, a fraction of an inch at a time. I could only get about a one-quarter turn on them before I had to reposition the screwdriver. Oh, what I would have given for my Black and Decker cordless screwdriver about then. Finally, I had one end of a board free. I loosened the screws at the other end and was able to rotate the board away from the window. I did the same with the other two boards and now there was an opening I thought I could squeeze through. But, I couldn't get myself up high enough to get my head and shoulders through the hole. I needed something to stand on. Stymied, I looked around the room again. I wished my head were not aching so, it made it hard to think.

I took a little leap at the window, trying to swarm up the wall and out the window, but when my feet landed back on the floor I thought my head was going to explode. That would not work; I had to find something to stand on.

The building was still empty though. I went back over to the window and stared out, frustrated. So near, yet so far. All I needed was just a little boost. But, there was nothing, *nothing*, to stand on.

"Come on, stupid, figure this out, McGyver Maggie." When I worked in the intensive care unit at the hospital in Seattle, a couple of the nurses dubbed me that after an inventive TV character by the same name. It seemed I was always be able to figure out how to solve a mechanical problem; I was the person who could repair anything with a paper clip and some spit. But, that skill seemed to have deserted me now, when my life and Amy's could actually depend on it. I reached out and jerked at the boards that had been fastened across the window openings, thoroughly frustrated.

One of the screws I had loosened fell out and landed on the floor. I stared at it—this could be my solution.

Again I set to work with my little disk screwdriver. Soon I had all three of the boards taken off the window. Now to see if my bright idea was that good a one after all.

I stacked the three boards up against the wall. Each one was about two inches wide, this six inches might be enough of a step to give me the boost I needed.

I grabbed hold of the window sill and stepped up onto my board experiment. But, they skewed off to one side and fell down, leaving me dangling. I needed a way to secure them in place, if just for a moment.

I picked the screws up off the floor and looked at the ends. All right! They were the self-tapping kind, very sharp on the tips. I grabbed one of the boards that I had taken off the windows and replaced the screws in the holes on each end. I stacked the boards up against the wall again, then put the one on top that I had replaced the screws in. I kicked my shoe off and used it to hammer the screws into the wall. If this held for even a few seconds it would give me the help I needed to boost myself out the window.

I applied my little screwdriver, leaning hard onto it to get it to get the screw to go into the wall. I got just one turn accomplished when the little disk screwdriver slipped off the screw and my hand was raked across the screw head, leaving behind a curl of skin. The air around me was soon blue as I struggled to get the screws to go into the wall of the building. Finally, each one had caught and I had managed to take several turns on them, hopefully this would be enough to keep the boards in place for the instant I would need. The lower boards had fallen down while I worked getting the screws in place in the top board. I put them back in place. Now to try out my bright idea.

I crossed my fingers and said a little prayer for help. I grabbed hold of the window sill, taking as much weight on my hands as I could. I stepped on my board pile and this time when I stepped on the contraption it held.

With those inches of added height, I was able to push myself over the window sill. Now I was hanging part way out of the window, staring at the ground. It seemed very far away.

The rain continued to pound on the leaves above me and the water was starting to find its way through. Within minutes my hair was wet, but the cool felt good on my pounding head. Now, how was I going to get to the ground without breaking my neck?

I ooched my way out of the window, until I was lying against the outside of the building, my legs still dangling inside. My fingers almost reached the ground, but it was still too far to just drop. My head felt like it was going to split open and bright dots of light danced behind my eyes. I had to get out of this position soon or I would be unconscious. I squirmed out a bit further, now I could just touch the ground. It was time to do it; if I pulled my way much further out the window I would fall.

I stretched my arms out as far as I could, hoping I could support my weight for just a few seconds and avoid a direct hit on the top of my head. I wiggled, my thighs were now at the window sill and there were no bendy parts in them. "Okay," I whispered, "Here goes."

I gave one last wiggle and felt my legs sliding out over the window sill. I tried to curl my head under, but I was right up against the side of the building and my head had nowhere to go. My arms quivered as I fought to hold them straight.

Suddenly, my legs were out. For a split second I stood on my hands, then gravity took over. I went down like a felled tree, landing flat on my back.

The world spun around me in shades of green and I was lying face up on the ground. My lungs would not work, I could not catch a breath. The wind was knocked out of me. I closed my eyes and waited while my chest muscles spasmed and my rib cage bucked with the effort. I knew eventually my breathing would start, but the edges of my vision were getting very dark by the time I was finally able to suck in a breath. I lay still for a minute, pulling in air and waiting for my vision to clear. My next thought was what else had happened in my plunge to the ground?

Nothing really hurt. My legs moved when I told them to, so did my arms. The rain felt wonderful on my face. The headache, while still a monstrous presence in my head, had eased somewhat. I rolled over on my side, then carefully got to my hands and knees.

There was a small tree nearby; only good fortune had kept me from hitting it as I fell. I used it to pull myself to my feet. I looked around. I was alone and free. Now, to go get help. First, though, I would try and see if Amy was really in the building where Glen said he had seen her. And where *was* Glen?

CHAPTER 44

▼

Working my way through the now-dripping trees, I went over to the building Glen had pointed out to me earlier. This one had glass on the windows, but it appeared to be full of junk. I could see no sign of Amy or anybody else.

I looked over at the trailer. The lights were still on inside. I needed to get a peek inside; maybe that was where Amy was being held captive.

The first window I tried was on the side that faced out toward the driveway and looked into the phone-booth sized bathroom. There was just barely room for a tiny shower stall, small sink and a toilet. The door was open, but the angle was wrong, so I couldn't see into the rest of the trailer. Rats! I went around to the side where there was a small bump out, almost like a bay window. I could hear muffled voices. Somebody was inside. I crouched down and moved crab-wise up to the window. With the lights on inside and the light outside dim, both from the clouds overhead and the dense overgrowth of bushes and trees, maybe I could risk a peek inside without being spotted.

With the feeling that my forehead was six feet tall and sending off flashes of light, I slowly stood upright, hoping I would not be seen from the inside.

There were no curtains, but the glass was filthy dirty. I could just make out three people sitting at a table and I could see what looked like somebody lying on a couch. The person lying on the couch moaned and moved about.

"I told you to keep quiet," came the unmistakable sound of Ollie Krupe's voice.

"Okay, smart ass, now what do we do?"

"Watch your mouth, Ollie. I handled things up to now and I will continue to do so. Now, we…"

"Oh, yeah, Gunnison," said another voice. "You've done a great job. Not only do we have this piece of shit on our hands, but you drug that Jackson bitch here, too. Somebody's going to be looking for her."

I couldn't stop my gasp. I clamped both hands over my mouth and dropped down onto the soggy ground. That had sounded very much like Carl Rolley and he was talking to *Glen?* I had to hear more. I pushed myself back up and leaned against the side of the trailer right by the window. I didn't need to see inside; I was pretty sure I knew who was in there. But, I did want to know what they were talking about. Unless somebody stuck their head out into the bay window, they would not see me where I was crouched down and plastered against the outside wall of the trailer. I could hear well enough to understand most of what they were saying.

"…and I can handle her," I heard Glen say.

"But what makes you think she will keep her mouth shut?" that was Ollie's voice now.

"Because she knows her aunt's life won't be worth squat if she doesn't play ball with us."

"That might work," said Carl, "But what about this Amy chick? She's going to be harder to shut up."

Glen laughed, a sound I did not like. "Oh, her? Simple. She's despondent over the deaths of her parents; she has nobody to help her; she just gives up and throws herself into the sea? under a truck? who knows. I'll help her cook up a nice suicide. It'll take a couple of hours to set it up, though. You guys stay here and keep an eye on things. I'll be back when it's time to move out."

I stumbled away from the trailer. I had to get away from here and find help. If I didn't, Amy would die.

The driveway had seemed short when Glen and I first drove in, but now it seemed to lengthen ahead of me as I walked. My legs felt weak and shaky and my head continued to pound. I was soaked to the skin now and getting cold. All I wanted was to lie down and take a nap, but I knew that would be a bad thing. I trudged on.

The rain seemed to be easing off and the sky was lighter. I tried my phone again, but still no luck. I came around a corner and there was the paved road. Now I prayed for a car to come by.

A sound behind me sent me reeling into the bushes. I heard shouts and the sounds of doors banging open and shut. Then an engine revved and a car was coming out of Carl's place.

I froze in place, willing the branches to cover me. Out of the corner of my eye I could see Glen's car moving down the path toward me. He stopped and looked both ways before pulling out onto the county road. His car started to roll forward, good, he must not have seen me. Then I saw his head turn my way again and the car lurched as he slammed on the brakes.

"Maggie! Thank God. I have been looking all over for you." Glen got out of his car and headed toward me. "What are you doing out here?"

He was smiling and looked sweet and innocent. Running would be useless, he could catch me in a minute. Now to test my acting skills.

"I don't know what happened, Glen. I came over to see where Amy was, you did find her, didn't you? and the next thing I knew I was locked in an empty building with a huge headache." I said, fingering the lump on my head.

"The same thing happened to me," he said, rubbing his head, too. "Only when I woke up I was in Carl's trailer with Ollie Krupe sitting there looking at me. You were right, Maggie, Ollie is as crooked as they come. He and Carl engineered some way to make it look like Amy's parents drowned, then with the help of Ollie's wife, Melinda, they were able to forge all the necessary documents to gain control of all of the Armstrong's possessions. They sold most everything, except for the GEO Metro that Carl has, and split the money."

"Ollie *told* you all this?" I asked, my eyes wide and astonished. Don't puke, now, I muttered inside my head. You'll give away the show.

"Oh, yeah, he thinks he's pretty hot stuff. He offered me part of the take if I would help and I pretended to agree with him."

"Well, let's go get him, then."

"It's not that easy, Maggie. In the first place, we don't have any real proof, not that I couldn't get some." Glen pointed to himself and smiled. "I am a cop, after all." He then frowned, trying to assume a serious expression.

"Secondly, and most important, they have Amy," he went on. "They took her away with them out the back of the trailer where Carl had the car hidden."

I felt my stomach drop. For a minute I had forgotten about her. "What do you mean?"

"Ollie told me that I had to convince you to just forget all about Amy and her parents and to go back home. He said if you don't, well, Amy could meet with an accident."

"But, Glen, Amy won't stop looking for her parents just because I'm not here," I said. "Aren't you afraid Ollie will do something to her anyway?"

"No, he's too much of a chicken. But, he will be able to convince her that they did drown, even if he has to pay somebody to be a fishing boat captain for a day and 'confess' to being the person with the boat that her parents fell off."

My tears were genuine. Amy would die, I knew that, and I feared for myself and Lola, too. "Can we go back to my aunt's so I can get into some dry clothes? Then maybe I can think better. I need some Tylenol for this headache, too."

"Of course, what's the matter with me? That knock on the head I got must have addled my brain. Here, let me open the door for you."

I sat in Glen's car, huddled as close to the door as I could manage. He was a liar and a killer and I didn't even like breathing the same air he did.

CHAPTER 45

▼

Glen pulled in Lola's driveway and shut off the engine. I hoped he was just going to drop me off, but no such luck. He followed me into the house.

Owen Grant was making coffee. Never had anything smelled so good.

"Dr. Grant, would you come take a look at my head, please?" I asked him, walking into my bedroom. He followed me.

"What on earth happened to you?"

"It's a long story. I don't feel like I'm fractured, but would you check, please?"

His fingers moved over the lump behind my ear. I clenched my teeth to keep from screaming, the spot was exquisitely tender.

"No, no fracture, I don't think, although I can't really tell without an x-ray. You have a pretty good hematoma there, though, and I bet it really hurts. What's going on around here, anyway? I seem to be having quite a run on blows to the head."

"You got that right," I said. "And yes, it hurts. Got any good drugs with you?"

He laughed. "Well, it couldn't be too bad, then, if you can make that kind of sense. Yes, I have a few hydrocodone that I can give you. Be careful, though, they can make you feel a little dizzy."

I washed down a tablet and glanced at my bedside clock. Twenty minutes, relief should just be about twenty minutes away.

"Did you find that Amy woman?" Owen Grant asked. "The FBI guy…"

I leaped to my feet and made a slashing motion across my throat. "Sssssssssh," I said, "Whisper, don't let Glen Gunnison hear you."

Owen looked at me, then whispered, "What's wrong?"

"We can't trust Glen, either," I whispered back. "He is in cahoots with Oliver Krupe and Carl Rolley. I'm pretty sure they killed Amy's parents and now they have Amy, too."

"How do you know all that?"

"Well, it's a long story, but the short version is this: I went with Glen to look for Amy at Carl Rolley's place. I got hit on the head and locked up in an empty shed. Glen did that, I'm sure. I managed to get out, then overheard Ollie, Carl, and Glen talking. They have Amy with them, but there was no way I could rescue her with all three of them there. I was trying to walk out to get help when Glen found me and brought me back here."

"But, he seems to be acting normally," said Owen.

"He's putting on a good show, isn't he? He told me that Ollie or Carl had knocked him out, too, and that now I need to just give it up and go home, that Amy would then be able to accept the fact that her parents drowned and everybody would be safe. That's what it will take to make them let her go, he said. Otherwise, he said he was afraid something bad would happen to Amy, too."

"What are you going to do?"

"I'm going to pretend to go along with Glen's suggestion. What did you start to say about the FBI guy?"

Owen looked at his watch. "He called about a half an hour ago to say that he was about two hours away. He is coming down here. He should be here in ninety minutes or so."

"Okay, then, here's what we do. Just follow my lead. I'm going to go and tell Glen that I'm going back to Spokane. We need to get rid of him before the FBI gets here."

Owen stood up. "Let's do it," he said.

"I don't think that's too bad a bump." Owen opened my bedroom door and spoke loudly. "Just let me know if you start to have any symptoms that scare you. I'll be here for another little while, anyway."

I followed Owen to the kitchen, where Glen was sitting at the table, sipping coffee. "I helped myself, if that's okay," he said.

I hope you choke on it, you snake, I thought, but said, "Sure. Well, I decided you were right. I have done as much as I could, but it looks like Amy's parents did drown after all. It's going to be really hard for her to accept that, but I'm sure that eventually she will. As for me, I'm going to pack up and head home. Thanks for all your help, Glen. I hope eventually you can do something about Oliver Krupe."

"Me, too," he said. "It's hard to work with someone you know is a crook. Maybe by the time the next election rolls around I'll have a chance to unseat him."

Just leave, leave! I screamed inside my head. "Thanks for bringing me home, Glen. I'm going to go lie down for a bit now; my head is killing me."

"I'm going to go check on Lola, then I should be on my way, too," said Owen Grant.

Glen stood and stretched. "I better go. Amy will need my help to deal with all this stuff once she's free. I have to go to the office and check on Jim, too, he's not used to coming in so early and he's probably asleep on the job. I'll get my car out of your way, Owen." Glen turned and winked at me, he had bought my act.

Owen Grant and I stood and watched Glen drive away. Owen walked out to his car and got in. He watched until Glen's car was out of sight then came back to the house.

"I'm not going anywhere," he said, "At least not until that FBI agent gets here. I'll be right back." Owen went out and got in his car. He backed out of the driveway and turned the opposite way from the direction Glen had gone.

Within just a few minutes he was back.

"Hopefully if Glen was watching he saw me pull out," Owen said.

"That was a good idea," I said. "I'm glad you can hang around. I was going to ask you to, anyway. I think I will go lie down and give those drugs a chance to work. I heard Glen say it was going to take him a couple of hours to 'arrange' Amy's suicide, so we have a little time. If I happen to go to sleep please wake me up when Agent Randolph gets here."

CHAPTER 46

▼

When I laid down it was gray and raining. I didn't really feel sleepy, but I must have slept, because the next time I looked out the window by my bed the rain was no longer coursing down glass and sunshine streamed in. Henry was at the foot of the bed leaning toward the door, ears and whiskers forward. Whatever he heard must have been what woke me up. I had a moment of panic until I realized I had only slept for about a half an hour or so. But, now I needed to pull myself together and get moving, Amy's life depended on me.

I sat up slowly, holding my head in my hands. Owen was right; I was a touch dizzy from the hydrocodone, but the pain had eased off to just a dull memory. I stood up and opened the door. Henry ran out like a black streak and I could hear voices. Maybe Special Agent Randolph was here.

I walked out into the living room just as Owen handed a slim, dark, man the packet of papers I had left. I had never seen a real FBI agent before and I was somewhat reassured that he was not wearing what I thought was the requisite black suit, white shirt, and skinny black tie. Instead, he looked ready for action in tan Dockers, a short sleeve shirt, and Nikes. He tossed a light jacket aside then sat down and started to go through the papers.

"Agent Randolph? I'm Maggie Jackson, I called you earlier today," I said, easing myself into a chair. "You made good time getting down here."

The man stood up to shake my hand, then sat back down. "Nice to meet you, Maggie. I'm Special Agent Edward Randolph, but please call me Ed. Once I told my super about the kidnapping I had a State Patrol escort and we flew down the highway. Looks like you have quite a bit of info for me."

"Yes. There is a lot of stuff there for you to look at, but first we have to rescue Amy, she has been kidnapped and we are running out of time."

Ed's head snapped up. "Who took her. Do you have any idea?"

"Glen took her." Lola was standing in the doorway. Her color was good and she looked like she felt better than I did.

"Maggie, thank God you are okay" she said. "I heard Glen talking when you got home earlier, but I stayed in my room. He's the one who hit me over the head. Ollie was with him and they took Amy. I tried to warn you, but I couldn't talk straight."

"I know, I found her. I think it was Glen who hit me outside Carl's place. Then, he told me a tale about getting hit, too. Glen said after he came to that Ollie talked him into helping and told him he would profit by it, both with money and with keeping his job. Glen said that Ollie and Carl took Amy away again, but I don't believe him. I think she is still at Carl's. I told Glen a big lie about going home and giving up on all this and I hope he believed me. He left, anyway."

Ed's head was whipping back and forth between Lola and me like he was a spectator at Wimbledon. "What is all this about? Who's Amy?"

"It's all in my notes. But, the important thing now is to go and find her. It's the Sheriff, Oliver Krupe, his deputy, Glen Gunnison, and this guy named Carl Rolley who have her. They murdered Amy's parents and took all their possessions. I heard them talking—they plan to have Amy have an 'accident' like her parents supposedly did. We have to go and find her." By now I was up and pacing around the kitchen. Henry followed behind me, the fur along his back standing straight up.

"Hold on, hold on," said Ed, looking stunned. "So, you're saying that there are at least three guys who have this woman. Are they armed?"

"I would assume the sheriff and deputy are and I wouldn't be surprised if Carl Rolley doesn't have a gun or two around his place. Please, can we go look for her?"

Ed shook his head. "We can't go busting in on three armed guys by ourselves. I have a couple of handguns with me, but I can only use one of them at a time."

"I know how to shoot. Let me carry one of them," I said. I was hopping up and down with impatience. While we talked Amy could be breathing her last.

Ed looked at me for a minute, then sighed. "This breaks all the rules," he said, "But if you could come with us too, Dr. Grant, we might just have a chance. Do you have a weapon?"

"I keep a pistol in my glove compartment," said Owen Grant. "It's not safe around here after dark and not just from people. I have seen many a bear on my nighttime calls. I'll go get it."

Ed spent a few minutes showing me how to use the smaller of his two automatic pistols. My gun at home was a Smith and Wesson revolver. After he chambered the first round he told me how easy this little automatic pistol was to use—just flick off the safety and pull the trigger. He gave me a radio to carry also. My cell phone, now able to get a signal when it no longer mattered, would stay at Lola's. I didn't have a pocket to put it in, anyway, what with the gun and the radio to carry.

"I'm going to call the State Patrol and ask them for some more assistance," he said, pocketing his automatic and handing me an extra clip for the one I had. "There'll be no way for anybody else from the agency to get down here in any sort of helpful time frame. I want to have somebody for backup, though. Now, Maggie, you know where this Amy supposedly is being held? What's the place like?"

"It's kind of buried in the woods. They had her in a little travel trailer that looks like that's where Carl lives. There are several other buildings around, some almost all fallen down and a couple that are in pretty good shape. In fact it was one of those buildings I had to escape from earlier today."

"Okay, then, let's go. Maggie, you go with Dr. Grant and I will follow you. But when we get close, we need to find a place to pull off and leave the cars. We will need to go in on foot. We will need the element of surprise to pull this off."

"I'll have food ready for you all when you get back," said Lola, tying on her apron. "C'mon Henry, you can help."

Henry jumped down from the counter. He had needed a high vantage point to follow the discussion and now he followed Lola around the kitchen. "I'll be right back," I told him and kissed his nose.

Ed hung up the phone after updating the State Patrol and being assured of their help. We went out and got into the cars.

CHAPTER 47

▼

On the way to Carl Rolley's I filled Owen in on the rest of the story.

"I'm not surprised to find out that Ollie Krupe is crooked," he said. "I haven't really trusted him since his early days as a deputy; he was always working the angles and just skating on the edge of legal much of the time. Glen Gunnison's involvement really does surprise me, though. I always thought he was an honest young man. Now I wonder if this is their first venture into murder, though, there have been several deaths at sea recently."

"I think the most recent death that we could pin on them is that of Clarice Miller," I said. "She worked for Melinda Krupe in the town hall. Melinda was very angry that I had been given unsupervised access to the land records, Freedom of Information Act be damned! and I think Clarice paid for the blunder with her life. I just hope we aren't too late for Amy."

A half mile or so from Carl's driveway Owen slowed down and pulled into a wide place on the shoulder of the road. There was room there for both cars. We locked the doors and started walking.

The cars were still behind the trailer. That meant that unless they had all left in one vehicle, the men and Amy were still there. I saw that Glen's car was there, too. He was back with his gang of thugs.

Owen and Ed split up to circle around and come up to the trailer from the back. Ed told me to hide alongside the driveway. He gave me a radio to use to call out and tell the State Patrol dispatcher if anybody drove away. I found a tree stump buried in some bushes to sit on where I could peek out and see the driveway. Hopefully nobody could see me.

Time crept by. I did not have a watch, so I didn't really know how long I sat there, staring out through the leaves. I started to design a quilt in my head, but no green would be in it. I had my fill of green for the day. I heard a rustling in the brush behind me. There are lots of little critters that live in the brush around here and the only one I really feared would be a bear. I doubted one would come around this close to a human, but I stood up anyway and took Ed's gun out of my pocket.

It happened so fast I scarcely had time to be startled. One second I was holding the gun in front of me, the next second a booted foot flew out of the brush and kicked it out of my hand. I heard it skitter off through the leaves. In the next instant somebody had grabbed my arm and twisted it behind my back. An arm went around my neck, making it hard to breathe.

"So, you just had to come back and snoop around, huh?" Glen Gunnison snarled in my ear. "Couldn't take a friendly hint, could you. Well, friendly time is over, walk."

I stumbled down the driveway and across the clearing to Carl's trailer. Glen pushed me up the stairs and used my body to shove the door open. He threw me down on the floor by the couch where Amy was lying. I heard the handcuffs snick shut around my wrist and then to the leg of couch. It was bolted to the floor right in front of my nose.

The inside of the trailer stank of rancid cooking oil and sour sweat. Probably the smell of fear, too, I thought. Amy stared down at me, her eyes huge in her face.

"We'll be okay," I said, then gasped as a boot found its way to my side.

"You shut the fuck up!" Glen screamed. "Open your mouth again and I'll kill you right here, right now."

I shut the fuck up. Glen sounded like he was losing control. If Amy and I were to have a chance at all we would have to play by his rules.

"You get that boat lined up yet, Carl?"

"Yeah, Glen. He said he should be at the dock in about a half an hour then we can go out." Carl's voice was shaking. He sounded like he was as afraid of Glen as I was. "Where's Ollie, anyway? He went to the outhouse a half an hour ago."

"Ollie won't be coming with us, Carl. He decided to stay in the woods for awhile."

"What do you mean, Glen?"

"Well, let's just say it's only a two-way split from now on."

"Oh, God, you killed Ollie?" Carl sounded like he was almost in tears.

"It was his own fault," said Glen, "He was getting greedy, said he deserved more because that fat pig Melinda was involved too. This is better. I will be named sheriff and this place will be ours. Let's get our gear packed up so we can get going the minute we hear the boat is at the dock."

Glen and Carl began carrying things out to the car. I shifted around on the floor to try and get more comfortable. When Glen threw me down I ended up in an awkward position and my arm was going to sleep. But the new position was no better, there was a bump of something gouging into my side. Oh, the radio! Having kicked the gun out of my hand, Glen had not taken the time to look for more weapons and he didn't know I had Ed's radio. Ed showed me the steps to call the WSP dispatcher, but he also showed me what he called the panic button. He said if that button was pushed it would open a transmission line to the Seattle FBI office. Nobody would answer the transmission, but any noise close to the radio would be sent to the office, where it would be recorded as well as heard. There was also a built-in GPS in the radio and the FBI office would be able to pinpoint where the radio was. Maybe technology could save our lives.

Glen and Carl went back and forth, loading up the car. Every time they left the trailer I would inch my hand closer to my pocket. Finally, I had hold of the radio. I held it up to my face, trying to see the panic button Ed had pointed out. Carl opened the trailer door to come in for another load. The instant of extra light let me see the blue button Ed had shown me. I held my breath and pushed.

I couldn't see that anything had happened, except that a row of dashes started climbing up the side of the screen where the frequency that was being used was displayed. This motion kept repeating and I had to hope that I was now transmitting to the FBI.

"That's the last of it, Carl. Call your man again, we need that boat ready right now. Tell him to be sure and change the name, too."

Now I knew where The Sea Ghost had gone. This pal of Glen's and Carl's must be part of their scheme, too. They used the boat to get rid of anybody inconvenient and changed the name on it so it was untraceable. 'Gary Wilson' probably was just a one-time name use also. I could hear Carl's voice and assumed he was using the phone. I couldn't make out what he was saying, though.

"The boat's ready, Glen," Carl said, his voice continuing to tremble.

"It's about time. Now, help me get these bitches out to the car."

"Do we have to kill them, Glen? Can't we just leave them here?"

"You worthless piece of spineless shit. I should have known you'd turn into a wimp. No, stupid. How fast do you think they'd run to the cops, anyway? Come on, this will be easy. Just toss 'em in the water and let nature take its course. We aren't really going to kill them ourselves."

"I'm not a wimp, Glen." Carl's voice no longer shook. He sounded mad. "I just never planned on murder."

"Well, you sure didn't have any trouble taking care of the Armstrongs, now did you."

"That was their own fault. I couldn't get that old bag to agree to a boat trip, something about getting seasick, or something. Then the old man was getting wise to the fact that I had borrowed some of his things and hadn't brought them back. He wasn't going to shut up about it, so, bam."

I heard Amy gasp. She had heard what Glen and Carl said. I knew this was the truth, that her parents were indeed dead. But, where were their bodies? Had Glen and Carl thrown them in the ocean, too?

I felt a hand under my arm. "Get up," said Glen, unlocking the handcuffs. "Time to go for a little boat ride."

I struggled to get my feet underneath me and stand up. While I wrestled around on the floor, I managed to slip Ed's radio back into my pocket. I was glad it was a compact model, maybe it would go unnoticed.

Glen pushed me out the door and into the back seat of his patrol car; he must have swapped it for his personal car after he left me at Lola's. Like I had noticed before, there was a plastic partition between the front and back seats. In this car the door locks and handles were missing in the back, too. It was as good as being thrown in a cell. He went back in the trailer and came out with Amy. He shoved her into the seat next to me and slammed the door.

"Did you hear what they said, too, Maggie? Carl did kill my parents. We have to get out of here and find some help." She patted the door, looking for the handle to open it. "Where is the door handle, anyway?"

"This is a cop car, Amy. They take the locks and door handles off so a prisoner can't escape. That's why this partition is here, too," I said, knocking on the plastic.

"We're trapped," she screamed. "Let us OUT!" she yelled, kicking at the window.

"Don't waste your energy, Amy. We can't break out and they won't let us out, at least not until we get to the boat. I called the FBI and an agent came down after I told him about your parents and you being kidnapped. I met him at Lola's and he gave me a radio that has a panic button on it that is supposed to transmit to the FBI office. I managed to push it while we were in the trailer and I hope they have been listening to everything that's been going on. I hope that help comes for us soon, too. But, when we get to the dock, that's the docks in Ilwaco, if anybody can hear me. Glen and Carl will have to make it look like we are going with them willingly, Amy. Keep your eyes open for an opportunity to escape if we aren't rescued first."

As I talked, Amy calmed down. "Okay," she said, "But, what will we do?"

"I don't know. We'll have to play it by ear when we get to the boat. You know how to swim, don't you?"

"Yes, I do," she said. "Why, you think we should jump into the water?"

"It might be our only chance to get away. Ssssh, here they come."

CHAPTER 48

▼

"Why are we having to go to the docks at Ilwaco?" asked Glen, as he turned on the ignition. "I told him to pull up at Ollie's place or on the back side of the jetty."

I kept scanning the woods, willing Ed Randolph or Owen Grant to come out of the bushes, guns blazing. But, if they were watching, they probably would not try a rescue by themselves. Both Carl and Glen had guns and would use them, of that I was sure. I patted the radio in my pocket, praying its batteries were well-charged and it was transmitting.

"Dick said it's too rough out today to try and pull up to the jetty, Glen, and the tide's too low for Ollie's. But, he will go to the dock that is the farthest away from the main docks, so we should be fine. Plus, the parking lot by that last dock is somewhat secluded, so that will help, too."

"I guess that sounds okay. It's about time something went right. Another hour and we should be home free. You girls comfy back there?" Glen laughed at his supposed concern for our comfort.

I could feel the words coming and knew I would sound like a B movie queen, but I couldn't stop them.

"You won't get away with this, Glen. People knew where I was going."

"Oh, you mean like your senile old aunt Lola? I won't have any trouble taking care of her. Too bad she has had so much trouble lately remembering to turn off her stove, or her iron, or something. Too bad her house burned down and she couldn't get out."

Henry was with Lola. If I couldn't get myself free he would perish too. For an instant my vision went red. I would get free and I would make sure Glen got what he deserved. "Big talk from a small man," I said.

Glen laughed. "Sticks and stones…" he said.

Too quickly we were driving along the waterfront in Ilwaco. We passed the main docks that bustled with fishermen and tourists. Like Carl had said, the dock at the far end did have a parking lot surrounded by bushes. We would be virtually invisible.

"So what's the name of the boat today?" Glen asked. "And is it still the same color as before?"

"Yeah, Dick didn't have time to do any painting, but his boat looks like a hundred others; we won't stick out in the crowd."

Glen stopped the car. He opened the back door. "Now, get out nicely. Any funny business and you will die right here." He grabbed me and pulled me out. Carl came up and stood close to me, the barrel of his pistol jammed into my side.

"C'mon," he said, "Move it."

I walked ahead of him, watching Amy and Glen out of the corner of my eye. Her eyes were wide and staring; I knew she could feel the barrel of a gun in her side as well.

"There is it, last one on the left," said Carl. "Looks like he is calling her Problem Solver this week."

"That's appropriate for us," laughed Glen. "Dick has a sense of humor, I'll give him that."

The boat was near the end of the dock. Maybe if we could jump in and swim…I looked at Amy. She reminded me of a deer in the headlights, standing frozen in the road and unable to move as a car bore down on it. She wouldn't be able to make the move, I was sure. I would have to and hope that I could and then get some help before they hurt her.

The four of us walked down the swaying dock, struggling to keep on our feet. Carl had been right, the sea was rough today. I wondered if they were even letting smaller boats over the bar out into the ocean. Maybe the Coast Guard would intervene if we tried to go out.

The dock was a fairly long one, but we were finally at the boat. I could see where ropes had been fastened to the floor in front of a bench seat that ran along one side. They would probably tie us down so we couldn't get away. Glen waved at the man that I guessed must be Carl's pal, Dick, and he said, "Welcome aboard." It was Dick Medcaff, Eve's abusive husband. I was too scared to be shocked, but hoped he could be brought down, too, and Eve could start to have a decent life.

Carl nudged me forward. It was now or never. I pretended to stumble, and threw my arms out to balance myself. For an instant Carl's gun hand was knocked aside and I tripped over the edge of the dock and into the oily water.

I kicked as hard as I could, pushing myself as deep into the water as possible. I forced myself to open my eyes, too, cringing at the salty sting. I fought the moving water, grateful for the daily swimming I did at the gym in Spokane. Once I was under the dock I floated to the surface. I took in a careful breath, trying to be quiet.

"I have to find her, Dick," I heard Glen raging. "We can't let her get away. Carl, here, take over with this other bitch and don't let her get away from you. Put her in the boat and tie her down. I'm going in the water."

Great. That's just what I wanted to hear. I swiveled my head around. Pilings were everywhere, but it wouldn't take Glen long to find me if I stayed put behind one and he would see me if I moved. The boat above me was rocking back and forth and I could hear thumping and banging noises. Other boats were coming and going from the dock. I could feel the vibrations of their propellers in the water. It was cold, too. I wouldn't be able to stay in the water very long. I heard footsteps on the dock above.

"I'll be right back. She can't have gotten far."

Glen would be in the water in an instant. Frantic, I looked around again. There, at the end of the dock near the beach, what was that? I headed toward shallower water and land, pulling myself from piling to piling, trying to stay invisible. I heard a splash, that must be Glen jumping into the water. I tried to move faster.

I looked back and caught a glimpse of Glen. He was moving through the water, circling each piling as he went. He was heading toward me and I could see that he had taken the time to put on a wet suit. He would be able to stay in the cold water much longer that I could. I took a deep breath and slipped under the water, again subjecting my eyes to the sting. I could see the beach, there was a steep drop off and something hanging in the water there.

As I got closer, I realized what I was seeing was an overturned rowboat, probably abandoned there, from the look of it. Praying that it was not totally submerged, I pulled myself underneath it and let myself float to the surface again.

I felt my head come out of the water. I was under a wrecked rowboat, its stern end bobbing up and down in the water. I could see bits of the sky through the splits in the bottom of the boat, which now was a ceiling over me. Even better, I could see that there was land under the other end, I might be able to crawl up on it and get out of the water.

I was shivering so hard it was all I could do to pull myself onto the sand. It was wet, but not as cold as the water had been. I also noticed for the first time that it was warm under this old boat; the sun was shining on it and warming up the air underneath. Spider webs sparkled in the sunshine that came through the cracks. I could almost feel the little feet as the spiders dropped down on me. But, I was too big for the web, maybe they would leave me be. I felt other things falling on me and willed myself not to thrash wildly about, although that is what I wanted to do. I forced myself to lie still and for a few minutes did so, waiting for the warmth to penetrate my wet clothes and stop the shivering.

CHAPTER 49

▼

Miraculously, Ed's radio was still in my pocket. I pulled it out, expecting it to be dead. But, I was amazed to see the little line of dashes continuing to race up and down the side of the screen.

"I am under an old rowboat at the end of the farthest dock to the south at the docks in Ilwaco," I told the radio, hoping somebody was listening. "Glen Gunnison and Carl Rolley have Amy Sanders and they are going to take a boat called the Problem Solver out into the ocean. I think their plan is to throw her out of it so that she will drown. They had the same plans for me, but when we got out on the dock I jumped into the water and got away from them for the time being. If Glen doesn't get to me first, I am going to try and get out from under this boat and go find the Ilwaco police. But, if he does get me, or if they decide to take Amy out anyway, notify the Coast Guard to stop the boat. Tell them that both Carl and Glen have guns, though. I hope you can hear me."

I put the radio back in my pocket. The shivers had stopped and I felt somewhat warmer. Now, to get out of here.

I pushed up on the end of the boat that sat on the land. It did not budge. I had no way of telling how much of it was buried in the sand, but it was too heavy to lift. Had I been able to get my feet under me I might have been able to push it up using my legs. But, all the Gravitron workouts notwithstanding, my upper body strength was still not enough to allow me to lift the boat while lying flat. I would have to go back in the water.

I clenched my teeth. I knew how cold it was going to be and it met all my expectations. Hoping I could get back out before I start to shiver and shake again, I pulled myself to the end of the boat that bobbed in the ocean. Before I went under the boat and back out into the open water, I stopped to peek out through a crack in the stern of the rowboat. Glen was still searching pilings, but he was off to one side. If I could slip out from under the overturned boat on the side opposite him, I might be able to get out onto the land without him seeing me. I took a deep breath and pushed myself under the water.

I felt my way under the side of the boat and pushed my way to the surface. I was cold again, but at least all the bugs I imagined had dropped onto me should have washed off. Glen was not in sight, but I knew I might only have a few minutes. As quietly as I could, I moved through the water. The curve of the beach and the docks had slowed down the storm waves and the water was calmer here, but I was grateful for the little bit of wave action that pushed me toward land. I wormed my way onto firm ground again, grateful for all the overgrown vines that wound above me. I crawled up beside the boat and into the bushes. If my bump of direction was being true, that parking lot should be ahead of me somewhere. I would have to stay low, though, or Carl or Dick would see me from the boat.

I crawled up a slight incline, fighting vines and then bramble bushes. If I did get out of this alive I would look like I'd been trapped in a sack full of cats. These bramble thorns were mean. I could feel trickles of blood on my face and arms and legs from lots of scratches. Finally, I saw the parking lot in front of me. There was a four-wheel-drive Chevy pickup parked there, its body high off the ground on oversize tires. I slid out of the bushes and onto the asphalt under the truck. I lay my head down and sighed. The warmth felt delightful. I soaked it up for a minute or too, but I knew I had to get up and find help. I rolled to the edge of the truck and froze, that was Glen's voice I heard.

"No, I bloody well did not find her, goddamn it anyway," he said.

It sounded like he was standing right by the truck. Carefully, I turned my head and looked. No feet. He must be on the dock; sound carries funny around the water sometimes.

"So what are we going to do?" this was Carl's voice. He sounded like a demanding three-year-old. "We can't let her get away."

"I know that, you stupid fuck. The water may have taken care of things for us, though. It's pretty cold and she probably wasn't that good a swimmer."

Ha! I thought, a lot you know, asshole.

"Let's get underway, Carl. Tell Dick to take us out. We'll get rid of that Amy bitch, then come back and look for the body here. When we find it, we'll just take it out to sea and dump it too. C'mon, let's get moving."

I rolled out from under the pickup and looked toward the docks. I could see Glen and Carl walking toward the Problem Solver. They had been fairly close to me at the end of the dock closest to the beach. I was warm now, but I shivered anyway. I waited until Glen and Carl were on the boat and they had pushed away from the dock. Now, to find some help.

I hurried out of the parking lot and headed towards the busy part of Ilwaco, my shoes making squishy noises and squirting out sea water as I walked. I should be able to find a policeman or somebody there.

And there help was, standing with one foot up on a short piling, watching all the activity in the marina.

"I need some help," said, startling him. He jumped, then turned to face me.

"You certainly do," he said, reaching for his radio. "You sit down, I'll call for help."

I must really look bad. So what, it was Amy I was worried about. "No, not for me. This woman and I were kidnapped by a couple of guys, it's a really long story, but they planned to take us out onto the ocean and toss us overboard. I managed to get away and swim to shore, but they still have the other lady. There they go now." I pointed out into the harbor, where I could see the Problem Solver moving out into the open water.

The cop stared at me. "What do you mean, kidnapped?"

I was almost jumping up and down with frustration. "See that boat?" I said, ignoring his question. "That blue and white one named Problem Solver? My friend, Amy Sanders, is being held prisoner and they are going to kill her. We have to stop them. Can you call the Coast Guard, please?"

"No need for me to call. They aren't letting any boats that small cross the bar today. See how high the surf is running out there?"

Indeed, I saw a couple of boats head back to the docks after being hailed by a Coast Guard boat. But, the Problem Solver motored on, going faster now.

"They aren't going to pay any attention to the Coast Guard. They are trying to get out anyway. The whole area can't be patrolled at once. Please radio the Coast Guard." I said, pulling on the cop's arm.

"You may be right. They don't look like they are going turn back." He pulled his radio off his belt.

I heard him talking, saying something about stopping the Problem Solver before she got over the bar. I saw the Coast Guard boat change direction and head toward where the Problem Solver was heading out over to sea.

They were so far away by now it was like watching toy boats bob in a toddler's bath. The Problem Solver's bow rose up in the air, Dick had obviously opened the throttle all the way. The boat zipped along the water then suddenly flew into the air and came down with a huge splash. They had made it over the bar and were out in the ocean proper.

The Coast Guard boat followed. I couldn't really see or hear anything from the docks, but I assumed they were hailing the Problem Solver, trying to get her to stop. I heard the whup-whup-whup of helicopter blades coming up behind me. I was gratified to see that this was a Coast Guard chopper. It too headed out to sea.

Dick must have really had to fight the waves, but the Problem Solver was getting smaller and smaller, they were able to get further out to sea. The Coast Guard boat followed them, bouncing about in the high waves.

The Coast Guard boat suddenly veered away. I could see tiny flashes of light from the Problem Solver and imagined I could her the gun shots I was seeing. Smart. Carl and Glen were shooting at the Coast Guard.

The helicopter dropped low and I saw more flashes of light from the Problem Solver. If one of those shots connected, the copter would go down. The pilot pulled up and hovered high enough to be clear of flying bullets.

Now the Coast Guard boat was approaching again. This time I saw flashes of light from it, too. They were returning fire.

Suddenly the Problem Solver turned hard to the north. She almost capsized in the waves, but then straightened out and started to move away from the Coast Guard boat. The Coast Guard continued to follow her, though. Glen and Carl continued to shoot at the Coast Guard and the Coast Guard continued to shoot back. I was shaking hard. If Amy didn't drown she would probably be shot to death.

A large crowd had formed on the waterfront. This was like a movie gone real and they were ohhing and ahhing as the chase continued. I could see things flying out of the boat as it bounced in the rough water. The flashes of light continued to come from the Problem Solver, too. Then I saw the Coast Guard fire again. A few seconds before I heard it, I saw a huge billow of yellow flames and smoke rise up from the Problem Solver and it disintegrated before my eyes. I could see flaming pieces of boat rise up into the sky from the fireball below, then drop back into the water. One of the Coast Guard shots must have hit the fuel tanks or something.

I dropped to the ground, sobbing. Amy was dead, so were Carl, Dick, and Glen, although they were no great loss. So many people gone, and it was all my fault. How could I ever face myself again?

"Look!" I heard somebody yell. "What's that guy doing?"

I forced myself to stand up and look out to sea again. Maybe the people had been blown free and were being rescued? I looked to where bits of the Problem Solver continued to burn as they floated on the water. The Coast Guard boat bobbed nearby, but seemed to just be watching. Off to my right, though, a I could see the helicopter dropping down closer to the churning ocean. A man in a bright yellow wet suit was riding a cable being lowered from the helicopter.

When he was low enough, he dropped off the cable into the water and started to swim. Within seconds, he was swimming back to where the cable dangled about him, pulling something behind him. Motioning the pilot to lower the cable, he grabbed hold of it. I could see he was holding what looked like another person. They bobbed about in the water for a few minutes while he struggled to secure this person to the cable. Then he made a motion with his hand and the helicopter began to pull the cable up. As it rose, I saw something small drop back in the water. Now all I could do was wait along with everybody else. The diver was next pulled out of the water and the helicopter headed toward the beach.

The helicopter landed a short distance away. I hurried to get to it, hardly daring to hope. Yes! That was Amy they had pulled out of the water; I recognized the pink pants she had put on at Lola's so many hours earlier today. They helped her to the ground and she stood looking around, the dazed expression of earlier gone. I pushed through the people who had run up with me to watch the helicopter land. Amy saw me and ran my way. She threw her arms around me.

"Maggie! You're okay! They told me you were dead, so I wasn't going to let them kill me too."

I hugged her tight. Yes, she was real. "Yes, I'm okay, I think. But how in the world did you get away?"

"Well, Carl and Glen started shooting at the Coast Guard boat and they were going to try and get away. Glen told Carl to throw me overboard, and he did. But, I was holding onto a seat cushion and wouldn't let go. He finally just pushed me into the water, seat cushion and all. I just barely got away before I heard this big explosion. Then, the helicopter picked me up and I didn't let go of that seat cushion until I was up out of the water. Did they get Glen and Carl and Dick?"

"Sort of," I said, trying to stem my tears of relief. "It looks like one of the Coast Guard's shots hit the gas tank or something and the boat blew up." We looked out to sea, where the Coast Guard chopper continued to circle the area where the Problem Solver had exploded.

The diver who had rescued Amy went back into the water and we watched as he swam around a little and was picked up by the cable again, empty handed. The helicopter banked, then flew off to the north. It didn't look like they had found any more survivors. I was glad, in a way. Glen, Dick, and Carl deserved to die for all the lives they had taken, but I sort of wanted them to rot in jail for years and years, too.

"Let's see if we can find somebody to give us a ride back to Lola's," I said, finally able to let go of Amy. "I want to get the Blazer and go back to Carl's to check on Owen Grant and Ed Randolph. I hope they are all right. I haven't seen them since we split up."

I saw the policeman I had talked to earlier and led Amy his direction. I was pretty sure he'd be happy to be our taxi.

A roaring engine and squealing tires stopped me before I got to him. Before the car stopped rolling Owen Grant leaped out and ran over to Amy and me.

"My God, Maggie, you're okay. And Amy too. What a relief."

Ed Randolph jumped out of his car and ran over to us, a huge grin on his face. "Good work, Maggie! You were able to transmit from my radio and the cavalry arrived. There is a mob of guys going over Carl's place right now. What happened here, anyway?"

The policeman walked up to Ed and introduced himself. They stepped away from us to huddle and talk. I let the policeman tell Ed what happened from his standpoint; I hoped my story would wait until I could get into some dry clothes.

Ed thanked the Ilwaco policeman and shook his hand. It looked like their conversation was finished, for now. He told him he would get back to him for a signed statement and then he came over to us.

"Can we go back to Lola's, Ed? Both Amy and I need dry clothes and we're hungry. Then we'll tell you what happened in Carl's trailer. Did you send somebody to pick up Mrs. Krupe also?"

"Sure, we can go back to your aunt's. We can talk there as easily as here." Ed opened the back door of his car and Amy and I crawled in.

"Sorry about your upholstery," I said. "Oh, by the way, here's your radio, just slightly the worse for wear."

"Thanks, Maggie. This little radio sure earned its keep today. And don't worry about the car seats, they will wash."

CHAPTER 50

▼

The ride to Lola's was quick and even though I didn't know if I ever wanted to get wet again, the hot shower felt pretty good. I could hear Lola rattling pots and pans around in the kitchen. I knew the feast she had promised us earlier was ready. I hadn't realized how hungry I was until a whiff of her lasagna drifted into the bathroom. I could hardly get dressed fast enough.

Soon I was at the table with Ed Randolph, Owen Grant, Amy, and Lola. We all ate until we were gasping with pleasure. We then waddled into the living room and found comfy spots to sit. Lola offered coffee and the rest of the cookies I had baked.

"Okay," said Ed, wiping chocolate off his mouth. "I think I'll live. Now, if you don't mind, I would like the whole story, starting with you, Amy. I'm going to tape this, if that's okay with everybody. I don't want to forget or overlook anything."

Everybody nodded, taping was fine. He set up his recorder and nodded at Amy. "Go ahead."

After a couple of unsure glances at the spinning reels, Amy started her story. Soon the recorder was forgotten. She started with telling Ed how her parents had always wanted to retire near the ocean and decided on the West coast after some friends' recommendation. She told him about their car, truck, trailer, and the piece of property they fell in love with. Then she went on and described how she had been invited to come for a visit, but found them gone.

"And I couldn't get that sheriff to help me at all," she said, fighting tears. "He just kept saying they had just gone away. Then, I met Maggie and told her my story. She offered to look around and, well…" Amy spread out her hands. "You pretty much know the rest."

"Yes, we know how things ended, but I'm still not sure of all that went on in between. Maggie, what can you tell me?"

I told Ed about my talking with Amy's parents' neighbors and the poor reception I had gotten from then and at the sheriff's office. He already had copies of all the papers and I gave him the typewriter ribbon, telling him what its significance had been. I also told him about getting information from Marty Adams in Spokane, and gave Ed Marty's number. I knew they would be talking, too. Then I told him what my time in Carl's trailer had been like.

"I hope the transmission got through with the part about Carl killing Amy's parents, too. She really needs to know for sure what happened to them."

I glanced over at Lola. She had been sitting twisting her hand in her apron pocket and she looked troubled. She caught my glance and sighed.

"Amy, there is something I need to tell you," she said. I think Ed knows about it already, but…" She pulled her hand out of her pocket. "Amy, do you recognize this?" Lola held out a ring, actually two rings, an engagement ring and a wedding band that had been fused together.

Amy's face crumpled as the rings dropped into her hands. "Oh, yes, these are my mother's. Where did you find them?"

Henry had been sitting quietly on the arm of the sofa. Now he went over to Amy and crawled into her lap. He gazed up at her with soft yellow eyes and said, "Maiow." She picked him up and he hugged her around the neck, his nose tucked into one of her ears. I could her him purring from where I sat. Amy wrapped her arms around him and held him close.

"I didn't actually find the rings," Lola said, "Henry did."

"But, where, how?" I wanted to know.

"While you were all gone he got very restless. After I got the lasagna in the oven I decided to take him out for a walk. He let me put him in his harness and everything," Lola said. "We walked around on the beach and he was really enjoying himself. So much stuff had been washed in by the storm there was lots to sniff at. We walked up the peninsula a ways and I could see where some of the tules had been washed away; the tide had been extremely high after the storm. I sat down on some driftwood to rest for a minute and let Henry's leash out so he could explore.

"You know that funny meowing, howling, noise he makes when he has 'killed' something, Maggie?"

I nodded. Boy did I ever know that noise. Nearly every night just after I go to bed he starts yowling around in the living room. It sounds like he is saying 'Hullo, hullo?' over and over. Then, he starts a odd moaning, snarking, noise and I can tell he is carrying something. His favorite "kill" is an empty toilet paper tube. He jumps up on the bed and deposits his prize in front of me and meows loudly, waiting to be praised.

"Well, he was poking around in the tules and started making those sounds. When he came over to me, he dropped the rings in my hand," Lola said. "He was very proud of himself.

"I wasn't sure what to do, so I went over and looked where he had been rooting around. I saw what looked like an arm, like an elbow, maybe. I scooped up Henry and ran back here as fast as I could. By the time I got back, the FBI men were here. I sent them to go check it out."

She turned to Amy and took her hand. "It was your mom and dad," she said. "Your dad actually still had his wallet in his pocket. I'm so sorry."

Amy leaned into Lola's side and I could see tears falling. I felt my own eyes fill. There had been too much today. I hoped Amy was strong enough to make it. I felt very close to losing control myself.

"I knew they were dead, Carl said so," she sobbed. "Now I'm just glad to have found them at last. Where are they?"

Ed had gotten up while Lola talked and was using the phone. He hung up and came back and sat down. "Our men recovered your parents. It looks like they were buried in the sand, but the storm washed the sand away enough so that Henry and Lola could see them. We took them to the hospital and they can stay there until you make arrangements. With both Carl and Glen dead, and of course we found Oliver Krupe's body at Carl's place too, there will be no need for an autopsy. We know how they died based on what Carl said in the trailer. Yes," he said when I looked the question at him, "The radio caught almost everything that anybody said; good job getting it transmitting. Glen had tried to make Oliver Krupe's death look like a suicide, but he did not do it very well. It was obvious Oliver had been murdered."

Amy lifted her head. "Thank you. I'll let you know what I want to do when I have figured it out."

"Okay, now it's our turn to listen to you," I said to Ed.

Ed opened his mouth, but before he could say a word Amy stood up. "I'm going to go lie down for a while," she said, putting Henry down in my lap. "I'm exhausted. Now that I know about mom and dad, I don't much care to hear about anything else bad. Thanks for the great meal, Lola. If I don't see you again this evening I'll see you in the morning."

Ed waited until Amy was gone, then he said, "As you know, Glen murdered Oliver Krupe at Carl's place. We found his body in the outhouse behind the trailer. We also found lots of stuff in Carl's trailer. He wasn't too bright, that's for sure. He kept purses, wallets, and billfolds from his victims, souvenirs, I guess. We have been working on several missing persons cases up and down the West coast and I'm thinking our discoveries in Carl's trailer will clear up several of those. We don't know much about this Dick, Medcaff is his last name, that owned the boat they were going to throw you and Amy out of, Maggie, but we suspect this has been their modus operandi right along; take people out to sea and drown them. There have actually been reports of several people falling off fishing charter boats, but all the boats and their owners have different names. We are going to be looking for as many of the named boats as possible, but I have a feeling most will not be found. It was probably the same boat used over and over."

Lola gasped. "Did you say Dick *Medcaff*?"

"Yes," said Ed, looking at his notebook, "That's right, why?"

I looked over at Lola. "You know Eve and Dick Medcaff, don't you? Eve told me you had helped her out a couple of times when things got rough at home."

"Yes," Lola said, "I do know Eve and Dick. He was not very nice to her and had her pretty well under his thumb. I was worried about her; I was afraid she was on the verge of being a abused wife."

"That's the impression I had gotten too," I said, "On the day we talked in the library. She wondered how she could survive if she were to leave him and I told her the same way she had survived before. I guess now she will have to figure that out."

"She won't have to do it by herself," said Lola. "I'll call her as soon as you think I can, Ed."

"We have talked to her, so anytime you want to go see her is fine. She did say that her mother was going to come stay with her for a few days until all the arrangements are taken care of, so she should be okay for awhile."

Lola nodded. "Good. I'll stop by in a day or two, then."

"Well, that's about it." Ed Randolph stood up. "Maggie and Lola, we are going to need signed statements from both of you. We'll get back to you in a few days for those. I can talk to Amy about her statement tomorrow after she has had a chance to rest."

"Ed, is there any way I could give my statements in your office in Spokane? I was supposed to leave for home today; I have a job and animals waiting on me. I need to get back."

"I don't see why that wouldn't work out," he said. "I'll give Spokane a heads-up on what's going on and an agent will call you."

"I have one more question for you," I said. "Do you know anything about that a Clarice Miller whose body was found in the water in Ilwaco?"

Ed nodded his head. "Boy, you were in all of this, weren't you? After we picked up Melinda Krupe she sang like a canary, hoping not to be in trouble for her part in her husband's schemes. She said that she thinks Oliver had Carl or Glen dispose of Clarice, after she told Ollie that she had let you look at those papers."

A wave of nausea went through my stomach. "So, her death I *was* my fault. I knew it."

"Not really," he said. "Sooner or later somebody would have done just what you did and discovered fake paperwork. Ollie's and Glen's scheme would not have gone on forever. You probably have helped save lives, actually. I don't think they were going to stop what they were doing; the money was too easy and too good."

"Thanks, I really appreciate that, Ed. Lola, I think I'll go to bed, too. I can hardly keep my eyes open and I am going to want to head home tomorrow." I wrote down my address and phone number for Ed, although I was pretty sure he already had them. I scooped up Henry and we went to our room for the night.

CHAPTER 51

▼

It seemed like I had just closed my eyes when the smell of frying bacon and the sounds of bird songs woke me. I stretched, luxuriating for a minute in the comfy bed. I was not really looking forward to the long drive home, but I would be glad to get there nonetheless. I rolled over and grabbed the phone.

"...so I should be home by late this afternoon, early evening, barring any trouble," I told Rick. "I am so anxious to see you and tell you everything."

"I'm glad to hear that you are okay. Your message yesterday was a bit confusing. I'll be wanting to hear the story, too. Sounds like your vacation turned into a bit of an ordeal."

"You have no idea," I said, staring at my soggy clothes piled on the floor. "Lola has breakfast ready, it smells like, then I'm going to pack up my stuff and Henry and head for home. I've missed you and I love you."

"I love you, too," he said, "Drive carefully and call me when you get in. I'll let Sully know you're on the way, too."

I got up and pulled on some clothes. "Let's get a move on, Henry. It's time to go home."

Epilogue

▼

Amy Sanders stood on a high bluff overlooking the ocean. The wind blew at her back, making her hair stream out on both sides of her face. She looked around and made sure she was alone.

This is probably against the law, she thought, but I don't care. Mom and dad always wanted to live by the ocean and now they will be here forever.

She opened two small cardboard boxes. Inside each there was a plastic bag full of a fine gray ash. She picked up the first box.

"Goodbye, mom. I will see you when I get there, too," she said. She pulled the bag open and let the ashes swirl out into the wind. They flew out over the booming surf below her feet and disappeared. She did the same with her stepfather's ashes.

Amy stood for a minute and watched the water, tears streaming down her face. Her tears gradually slowed and she smiled at the sight of two snowy white gulls, playing like airplane dog fighters in the wind. "I'm going home, now, mom and dad. Thank you for a wonderful life."

She climbed into her rental car and headed back to Lola's. She would pack up her things and head for home; at last her heart had found peace.

The End

Maggie's Mother's Chocolate Chip Cookies

Preheat oven to 350 degrees

Mix together (by hand is fine) in a large bowl:

½ c Crisco or other shortening (do not use margarine or butter, cookies will burn)
½ c sugar
½ c light or golden brown sugar, packed in the measuring cup

Add:

1 large size egg
2 T of brewed coffee or water
½ t vanilla extract

Mix together:

Scant 1 1/8 c white flour (don't use too much, cookies will be dry and hard)
½ t baking soda
½ t salt

Add to other ingredients in the bowl and mix well. Add small bag (6 oz) semi-sweet chocolate chips and ½ c chopped walnuts, if desired.

Drop onto ungreased baking sheet about 2" apart. Use a table teaspoon, like you would use to stir your coffee.

Bake for about eight minutes for soft cookies, up to 10 minutes for crisp. Watch out! They can get too brown fast.

Remove cookies from the baking sheets as soon as they come out of the oven and put them on a rack to cool. Store in an airtight container to keep them from drying out.

Instructions for making Amy's Irish Chain lap quilt

To make a lap quilt like the one Amy made, you will need about ½ yard of a dark fabric and about 1 ⅔ yards of a coordinating light fabric, or any two contrasting fabrics. These are the fabrics you will use to make 18 nine patch blocks and 17 of the plain, light fabric blocks.

First wash, dry, and iron your fabric smooth. Out of the dark fabric cut six strips of fabric 2 ½ inches wide. Cut five strips 2 ½ inches wide out of the light color. Then, cut 90 2 ½ inch pieces from the dark strips and 72 2 ½ inch pieces from the light. You will have some pieces of the strips left over after cutting out the small squares.

Be sure to sew an accurate ¼ inch seam. If you do not have a pressure foot this width, measure out ¼ inch from the needle and put a piece of tape down on the bed of the sewing machine to use as a guide. Sew a dark square to each side of a light square to make a strip three patches across, dark-light-dark. Make 36 of these. Next, sew a light square to each side of the remaining dark squares to make a strip three squares across, light-dark-light. Make 18 of these. Iron the seams toward the dark fabric.

Take two strips with two dark patches and one light patch and one with two light and one dark patch. Sew the strips together to form a 9x9 square checkerboard, the top row is dark-light-dark, the middle row light-dark-light, and the bottom row dark-light-dark. This will be one completed nine patch block, three rows of three patches each. Make 18 nine patch blocks like this. Each completed block should measure 6 ½ by 6 ½ inches. Press the seams toward the outside edges of the blocks.

Now take the light fabric and cut it into 3 strips 6 ½ inches wide across the width of the fabric. Then, cut this strip into 6 ½ squares. You will need 17 of these squares.

Now you are ready to assemble the center of your nine patch Irish Chain quilt. Take a nine patch block and sew a plain block to its right edge, placing the right sides of the blocks together. To the right edge of the plain block sew another nine patch. Add a plain block to the end of the row, then a nine patch at the end, so the whole strip is five blocks long. Make four strips like this.

Next, take a plain square and sew a nine patch to the right edge. Add a plain patch, then a nine patch, then a plain patch, so the whole strip is five blocks long. Make three strips like this.

Iron all the seams toward the plain colored blocks on each strip.

Next, take one of the rows that start with a nine patch square. Place a row starting with a plain patch underneath it and sew the rows together, lining up the seams between the plain squares and the nine patch squares. Use pins to hold them in place as you sew.

Add a row starting with a nine patch, then a row starting with a plain patch, until all the rows have been put together. Your quilt top should be five squares across and seven squares down when all the strips are put together.

See how the dark patches form criss-crossed lines? This is your Irish Chain!

Now measure down the center of your quilt, this should be 42 ½ inches. Cut two strips of fabric this length and 3 ½ inches wide in a coordinating color. (You will need about a 1 ½ yard if you want the frame piece to be seamless. Otherwise, cut 3 ½ inch pieces and sew them together end to end until you have strips long enough.) Sew a strip to both sides of the quilt top, making sure the seam allowances where rows of blocks are put together don't get twisted. Then measure across the top, this should be 36 ½ inches. Cut two strips of fabric 36 ½ by 3 ½ inches and sew one across the top and one across the bottom. This makes a frame for the center of your quilt. Repeat this step for your border, cutting strips 48 ½ by 6 ½ inches and sewing them down the sides, then 48 ½ by 6 ½ inches and sew these strips across the top and bottom. (You will need about 1 ²/₃ yard for a seamless border.)

Your quilt top should now measure 48 ½ inches by 60 ½ inches.

Make a back out of whatever fabric you like, even plain muslin. You will need about 3 ½ yards for the back and the same for the batting, unless the batting is 90 inches wide, then you will only need about a 1 ¾ yards. Cut the length of back fabric in half across the width of the fabric. Sew these two pieces together to make a back about 57 inches by 82 inches. Trim this to about 68 inches long. The batting needs to be about 52 inches by 64 inches. The top tends to stretch out and you don't want it to end up bigger than the batting or the back.

Place the back fabric on a flat surface, wrong side up. Center the batting over it, then center the top, right side up, on the batting. Pin the layers together and quilt as desired.

You can use either the frame or the outer border fabric for binding. You will need enough 2 ½ strips sewn together end-to-end (about 6) to equal about 220 inches of binding. This takes about ½ of a yard.

Consult a quilting book for full instructions on how to apply double-fold binding, or, if you would like illustrated instructions for a nine patch quilt block and the quilt above, along with instructions on how to attach the binding, send $7.50 by check or money order to:

> Karen Buck—Killer Quilts
> 8804 East Dalton Avenue
> Spokane, Washington 99212-2006

Contact me by mail or at Killerquilts@aol.com if you are interested in sending me your quilt to have it machine quilted. I also offer binding services if you want me to finish your quilt.

Copies of The Crematory Cat, the first in the Killer Quilts series, are also available at the above address for $15.95, which includes $2 for shipping.

0-595-33289-7

Printed in the United States
30630LVS00008B/127

9 780595 332892